MW01636074

The Brou-ha-ha

By the same author

The Rescuers
A Lease of Life
Victor and the Vanquished
The Child of Fortune
The Little Difference
Fido Couchant
Pity

P. B. Abercrombie

The Brou-ha-ha

Macmillan

SBN 333 13292 0

First published 1972 by
MACMILLAN LONDON LIMITED
London and Basingstoke
Associated companies in New York Toronto
Dublin Melbourne Johannesburg and Madras

Printed in Great Britain by
THE BARLEYMAN PRESS
Bristol

For Bill and Dido

Mrs Lamb to Mrs Nieman

c/o Mrs Bender,
27 Bede Street,
London, W.1.
April 1st

My dear Christiane,

You will probably be surprised to see the address I am writing from – I am a little surprised, and even alarmed, myself. But as Lord Byron remarked, there is a tide in the affairs of women which taken at the flood leads God knows where; though perhaps this is not a very complimentary description of Aunt Lucy's flat. The fact is that Harvey and I have decided to separate for a time. He has gone to New York as I told you he might, but I am not to come with him. I am very disappointed – I was so looking forward to seeing you, and to romping with you in the rural fastnesses of Jackson Heights. I do not know whether Harvey chose New York to go to without me specifically because he knew that I would be happy there – I hope not, because it would show a rancorous streak in his nature which I am sure was not there before, and I do want to leave Harvey at least as I would wish to find him. As it happens I do not want to leave him at all – it is all on his side; he cannot *stomach*, as he says, my infidelities. Apparently the man on the ship proved particularly indigestible. I suppose Harvey is not unreasonable when he asks me to change my entire character, but he does not realise how difficult it is. He has never tried to change his for the simple reason that there is so little room for improvement. He has lately begun bringing up my age, when he rebukes me. You are not a child,

Cornelia, he says, *at your age* one does not do such things. Most of these things have a lower age limit of about fifteen, and please God no upper age limit at all, but Harvey values dignity and order: certain behaviour is suitable to certain ages. He wants me to be *responsible*; so that, at the very least, when I have done something he considers reprehensible, I should feel guilty. Well, my conscience is like a sloth, asleep a lot of the time and usually upside down. I cannot feel guilty to order. And I cannot persuade him that it is useless to try to extract from me promises I won't be able to keep. He thinks it unreasonable of me not to promise, I think him unreasonable to ask me. So we are at an impasse, and with the true instinct of Government Service, Harvey has decided that when faced with one of *those*, one does not try to storm it, but simply goes round another way. We are to separate for six months or so. Harvey calls it 'standing back from the problem'. I do hope it will work – that in the canyons of Manhattan the man on the boat will dwindle into his proper perspective. As for me, staying with Aunt Lucy will be chastening. My patience and good humour will be severely exercised, and perhaps this moral gymnasium will tone up the underdeveloped muscles of my responsibility.

I suppose Harvey put Aunt Lucy up to inviting me here; certainly she pounced remarkably quickly after his New York job was finally settled. Before I knew what had happened I was installed here 'just till after Easter'. (Although every day is a holiday for Aunt Lucy and has been all her life, she sets great store by the feasts of the Church.) At first I felt resentful and doleful, suddenly finding myself in someone else's flat, without my own possessions; it is not even my own aunt. But at least it is comfortable; it is only temporary; and I will have time while I am here to look round at my leisure for something else.

I must tell you that Harvey's Aunt Lucy is a tall, rich, regal woman of 75 who collects poets, and who always has her own way. It is not altogether disagreeable to be a guest of Aunt Lucy's, but nevertheless almost everybody does resist at first and has to be overcome. She has immense powers of persuasion and command. One of her foreign friends, shortly after being introduced to her, remarked darkly, 'It is not she who bends.' She is immensely gregarious and considers it a disaster to sit down alone to a meal. This trait has caused a power struggle between herself and a series of housekeepers throughout the fifteen years she has occupied this house. The present incumbent, Mrs Lockett, although of frail appearance is in a strong position because she knew, when she came to be interviewed for the job, that Aunt Lucy had seen (and in many cases employed for short periods) every available housekeeper in England. Mrs Lockett is the last hope, until a new generation of housekeepers grows up, and this fact gives her more power over Aunt Lucy than anyone has ever had before. She uses this power in a fairly ruthless way. Dinner and lunch parties are strictly rationed, and it is dangerous to invite anyone unexpectedly to tea. Aunt Lucy relishes this bondage, contrasting it dramatically with those days, when she lived in the country, when she need never be without a tableful of guests and could enjoy delicious impromptu parties by merely sending a message to the kitchen, and perhaps going herself to see whether the butler had sufficiently extended the dining-room table.

Things are very different now, as Aunt Lucy frequently points out. 'They' are in control; the great struggle for power between servants and masters has temporarily gone their way. (My Aunt Lucy considers servants to be a race, not a profession.) But she is an honourable and indefatigable member of the resistance movement; she can harry the occupying power in countless ways, preparing for the day when they will be driven back into their attics and basements. I am, of course, to be her ally in this, but I cannot relish the battle. Mrs Lockett, a neat little woman with a concave face, has my sympathy and is often heavily outgunned. Preoccupation with this particular war, which one can never persuade Aunt Lucy is non-existent in nine-tenths of the modern world, is one of the mortifications of the flesh which is to refine my character.

Aunt Lucy is very upset about me and Harvey because for years she has held us up to her friends as an example with whom she can compare disparagingly the young people of today. Even to me she often says 'Look at Harvey' when she is asking herself rhetorical questions about why people cannot behave. She has always believed us to be perfectly devoted, and when we stayed with her in Gloucestershire she used to put us not only in separate rooms but on separate *floors*, lest sex should spoil our beautiful friendship. It is impossible to explain to her why Harvey has gone to New York without me. She thinks it very unwise, because in spite of her belief that sex does not really exist except in certain overheated imaginations, she thinks it is dangerous to leave a man alone anywhere for more than twenty-four hours. She shakes her head over poor Harvey, exposed to God knows what. I think she will write him a good many fortifying letters, and if I wanted Harvey to be punished I should be glad, as the deciphering of her writing is something which produces a pure and concentrated rage in the most amiable natures. I am patient, as you know, but I count it one of the blessings of my situation that I am not likely at the moment to get a letter from

Aunt Lucy.

Do write to me, Christiane. And would you ring up Harvey and ask him to dinner? He is staying at the Algonquin and in spite of Aunt Lucy's predictions will probably be having a pretty quiet life. I am sure you will like him, he is really very nice. As for me, I am going to improve myself while I am here – I shall go to all the galleries, read all the books, see all the good plays . . . This is beginning to sound like a speech by John F. Kennedy, and is just as full of sober resolution. I shall start at once with the National Portrait Gallery. I can foresee that I may want to spend a good deal of time somewhere other than here, and if Aunt Lucy objects I shall say I am trying to make myself more worthy of Harvey, which now I come to think of it is quite a good idea. Not that he will appreciate it – he thinks me rather erudite already and I am sure that if he had any say in the matter he would prefer me to concentrate on improving my morals. Perhaps while I am here I shall at least become more domesticated—Mrs Lockett may make me tidy if I remain under her influence long enough. I will leave you with this pious resolution. If you see Harvey, tell him I am determined to be good. I have at least put myself in an environment in which it will be difficult to be anything else.

My love to you, dear Christiane, and to Melville.

Yours, Cornelia

Mrs Bender to Sir Hugo Lamb

27 Bede Street,
W.1
April 1st

Dear old Fellow,

I am sending this by registered post as for some reason my last two postcards to you seem to have gone astray. As

I have not heard from you, I am afraid I have had to change my plans and have now asked Cornelia to come to me for a long visit. Poor child, she is feeling the separation from Harvey very much. I do not approve of it, as you know. I think it is madness to let a good-looking man like Harvey go alone to New York where any sense of morality is *quite* non-existent. However, I will not interfere, but I feel the least I can do is to give her a home. I daresay she will still be here when you come up for the Botanical Conference, and I am afraid you will find it *very* difficult to get into any decent hotel, but alas I cannot have you both – I would not *dare* to ask it of Mrs Lockett. It is a great pity you could not have been with me for Easter, after all it may be the last Easter we could have spent together. Do you remember the Simnel cake we used to have at home, and the cardboard egg with violets on it that I kept from year to year? And the Good Friday when poor dear Geoffrey fell out of the pear-tree and broke his arm? Those were the best days, before Geoffrey or I were married, when we were all happy together. Well, Hugo, you and I have only each other left, and perhaps soon that too will end. Dear old Father would be sad to see it. I would make the journey up to visit you if the weather were not so bad and if Doctor Dench had not forbidden it. I hope I shall hear from you *eventually*.

Ever your loving sister, Lucia

Mrs Lamb to Harvey Lamb

27 Bede Street,
W.1.
April 1st

Darling Har,

As you see, I am at Bede Street – I hope you approve. I don't know how long I shall be able to stand it, but I am sure Aunt L. will want me to stay until Uncle Hugo wants to come, so that she may have an excuse to refuse. He has been showered with postcards but has declined to respond, and must be punished.

She has put me in the *small* spare room, emptied all the cupboards but taken away the comfortable chair, from which I deduce that I am to stay a long time and spend very little of it away from the drawing-room. Nevertheless, you will be glad to know that I am remaining calm. I am saving money, and it is a good base from which to look for a new flat. I shall get something small and cosy, with just room for the two of us. I have not told anybody I am here – I just said I was going away. I am going to hibernate for a bit, and think. I miss you, I wish you hadn't gone to New York without me, but I hope the new job is interesting and that you will be an Ambassador in no time. I am *so sorry* I forgot to pack the trousers of your blue suit, I hope they arrived all right.

Aunt Lucy sends her love – so do I.

Yours, Cornelia

Postcard from Sir Hugo Lamb to Mrs Bender

Wood Cottage,
Pigpound Lane,
Pott Shrigley,
Chesh.

Acknowledge your registered letter. Once again, thank you for your invitation to London which once again I must refuse. I have a great deal on hand and shall probably be abroad for much of the year. I do not remember the occasion you refer to – I seldom think of the past as I have more important things to interest me.

Hugo

Mrs Nieman to Mrs Lamb

New York,
April 11th

Dear Cornelia,

I am sorry you don't come to New York, I have been looking forward to having you here. I have telephoned Harvey as you ask, and invited him for dinner. He sounds very suspicious; when I say I am a friend of his wife, he says 'My wife Cornelia?' as if he had several. I don't think he likes my accent. Perhaps your foreign service discourages its members from speaking to foreigners. I tell him what good friends we have been, you and I, how much my husband looks forward to meeting him and then on the instant I say General Carter comes to dinner on Saturday, I would so like you to join us. He says 'Well it is very good of you I shall be delighted,' and I am sure when he puts down the phone he runs to some directory to look up old Clive Carter. What an evening we shall have – I expect your Harvey and old Clive will enjoy themselves talking of war. When I tell Melville he is cross, but I tell him après tout Harvey must be nice if you chose him and at any rate will be handsome. Melville says 'So what?' He does not like to be reminded of the time it matters to him if men were handsome. I must ask some women for Harvey, there is an English girl in the apartment below, not beautiful but I think nice – she will do, and perhaps an American couple would be all right if they come from the East Coast? I am supposing Harvey to be a stiff-shirt. Perhaps I am unfair but it is best to be on the safe side. I will write again after the dinner party.

Yours, Christiane

Harvey Lamb to Mrs Lamb

Algonquin Hotel,
New York.
April 12th

My dear Girl,

Thank you for your letter of the 1st. I think it is an excellent idea that you should stay with Aunt Lucy. She is often lonely, and it is good to know that you are in comfortable quarters. I am a little concerned, however, by your reference to finding a flat of your own. Of course you must do as you wish about this, but it is no use your thinking in terms of our living together again, at any rate in the immediate future. Although my tour in New York may be a short one, it is very unlikely that I should be back in England for at least six months, and in any case you surely do not need me to remind you that we have agreed to separate for at least that length of time, and possibly as a permanent thing. I know it is your way to appear not to take things seriously, but I thought I had impressed upon you that we cannot go on in this way. I am not going to repeat to you my reasons for this decision, but I do want to emphasise that this break must be complete – it is the only way, however unpleasant it may be for both of us. We must stand back from the problem and give ourselves time to think about it; it was the constant changes in our relationship, I am sure, which made things so difficult for us in the past year. For this reason, I would rather that you did not write to me. You must of course, ask me for help of any kind if you should ever need it, but I do not think we should have any communication other than what is strictly necessary. I do not want to be unkind, but I am sure it is the best way.

I hope you are well, and are looking after yourself properly.

Yours, Harvey

Mrs Lamb to Mrs Nieman

Bede Street.
April 20th

My dear Christiane,

Thank you so much for your letter which by a strange coincidence was brought to me by the charlady who was late in arriving and told me it was because her husband had been queer in the night. I immediately thought of your troubles with Melville and she then gave me your letter, which she had brought up from the hall. Thank you so much for asking Harvey to dinner – I hope it will not prove to be only a *Christian act*, but that you like him, he *is* handsome and he can be very amusing when he chooses. I do hope he will fall madly – but temporarily – in love with the not-beautiful English girl downstairs. I have hoped for years for one small infidelity from Harvey, to even things up a bit.

Here, we are just recovering from last night's soirée. All our social occasions cover several days: a long and exhausting preparation, then the occasion, and then the winding down. Eight guests for sandwiches and Madeira may sound simple, but it represents quite a convulsion on the social seismic chart.

My aunt collects poets, but they must be clean and sober, and they must rhyme. She started with one, still the gem of the collection, called Spencer, and has added to him from time to time. Sometimes she reads or hears a poem and writes to the author telling him to come and see her, and extraordinarily enough, they often do. Sometimes they come only once, but there are several who have been regular visitors for years. Mrs Lockett regards them all with deep suspicion: when they have gone she counts the snuff-boxes. We have what Aunt Lucy playfully calls penny readings, when they get up in turn and declaim their own works. It is remarkable how many disciples of John Betjeman there are in this world. (John Betjeman himself came once, and admired the De Morgan). They are all extremely polite, running here and there at Aunt Lucy's call – *that* is one of the necessary qualifications. Last night a strange and sinister note was struck by the fact that somebody refused to read. He was a newcomer, the unlikely friend of a self-effacing and docile sonneteer; he seemed like a crow among doves. They tend to be fair or brown-haired and pale (probably from undernourishment), but this one was swarthy and lowering. His eyebrows met, and his eyes almost did too, I have never seen anyone with eyes so near together. When asked to read, he replied that he had not anything 'on him' and could never memorise his own work. Aunt Lucy insisted that he must read something, and chose for him 'Oh blackbird, what a boy you are, How you do go it!' He obeyed her, but he seemed like a man who eats sheeps' eyes to please an Arab chief. I suspect he may be the only real poet among them. His name is Fishtoft. He took sandwiches three at a time and drained his Madeira at a draught, putting the empty glass in a prominent position. Poor Fishtoft, he has not learned the rules of the house. Later on, he sidled up to me and muttered, 'Got anything stronger?' Perhaps he thought me a servant, or a 'companion'. Unfortunately I could not oblige him.

My role on these occasions is to hand round the sandwiches, listen, and smile. They are all inordinately polite to me and sometimes positively gallant. One, a somewhat fey young man with a pink face, a yellow moustache and blue eyes, as though done in poster paint, last night presented me with the poem which he had just read and which, as it is not long, I now append:

The song of the snail is silent

It has neither tune nor words
But it sounds as clear as a shout in your ear
To the early morning birds.

Aunt Lucy exhorted him to 'go on' when he had finished, and seemed affronted by its brevity and the fact that it was not 'serious', but I applauded, and was rebuked by Aunt L. for disagreeing with her. Afterwards, the young man pressed my hand and presented me with the manuscript, which I shall keep in case some American library should offer me something for it, when he has made his name.

Spencer is the only one among them with any pretentions to being handsome, and he is the acknowledged property of Aunt Lucy. He usually stays behind the others, and he and Aunt Lucy whisper together in the corner behind the piano. Last night the unlucky Fishtoft further damaged his chances by remaining too, perhaps in the hope of 'something stronger', or merely to outstay Spencer out of spite. Needless to say, he did not succeed in this. Aunt Lucy is the most expert mental bouncer in London.

I have nothing much to tell you about, except these innocent diversions, though I expect to keep up a flourishing correspondence with you while I am here; it is nice to leave the drawing-room occasionally because *there* one cannot read or even think without fear of interruption, but Aunt Lucy cannot do without human companionship and it is necessary to have a good reason if one is proposing to absent oneself. So I say firmly, 'I am going to my room to write letters' – and I always like to tell the truth where it is at all possible.

Tomorrow we are invited downstairs for a drink with Mr and Mrs Viot on the ground floor – they, of course, have the garden, and Aunt Lucy wants to get carte blanche permission to sit there whenever she likes. At present, she has to ask them each time and so far out of politeness they have been forced to agree. She always makes it quite clear that she does not want actually to be entertained – you must take no notice of me, you won't even know I am there! she says gaily, but on the last occasion, when I went with her, I did not think that she stuck to this side of the bargain. Her retinue consisted of me and Mrs Lockett carrying chairs and rugs, and she stationed herself in the very middle of the lawn (it is not a large garden) wearing a shady purple hat, and talked, lowering her voice to a dramatic but carrying stage-whisper whenever she thought 'they' were about. She made me read to her, 'Sotto voce, dear!' a peculiarly tedious historical novel, interrupting the narrative every quarter of an hour to move her conurbation of rugs and books into the sun. We ended up crammed into a corner, damaging the clematis on the wall. Then we had to creep into the house on tiptoe not, as one might have thought, to avoid reproach, but merely to add to the excitement of the occasion. She would not hesitate to ask again, but she wants to be able to go down whenever she likes, without this formality, and it involves having another key cut for the garden door. For all Aunt Lucy's powers, I am not sure whether she will succeed. Mr Viot shocked liberal opinion for miles around last Christmas by giving his wife a charlady wrapped in holly paper. I think – as did others – that this showed lack of heart, or at least of sensitivity, and although he has been asked several times to dinner, all Mrs Lockett's culinary skill lavished, and almost unlimited drink, I am not at all sure that he can be persuaded.

I must break off, dear Christiane, as I am bidden to go and listen with Aunt Lucy to part three hundred and ten of the Forsyte Saga. Love to Melville,

Yours, Cornelia

Mrs Lamb to Mrs Nieman

Bede Street.
April 22nd

Dearest Christiane,

I am writing again so soon after my last letter because a most extraordinary thing has happened – I met a friend of yours in the National Portrait Gallery! I was in one of those little claret-coloured rooms, do you remember? Probably not – I bet you haven't been there since we were at school. Well, in came this enormous man and stood in front of Byron. There was no one else in the room, or in fact I think in the gallery except the keepers; a few minutes later there he was again in another room, looking at Conrad. I went slowly round from picture to picture but he just stood there, looking at Conrad. When I got to him he moved back a little and said, 'Excuse me, madame, who is Tittle?' I told him that so far as I was concerned this was the only picture Tittle ever painted, then we talked about Conrad and then about other things. He told me his mother was Polish and that he lived in New York and in that inane way one does, I said, I have a great friend there, Christiane Nieman, and he went 'Ah!' with an enormous sigh like a lion yawning, as though he had discovered the solution to something – and then of course we started talking away like mad, and he turned out to be an Armenian, Tigran Leontyev – isn't it amazing? I have asked him to dinner at Bede Street on the strength of his being a friend of yours. When I told Aunt Lucy she said, 'Oh dear, I hope we shall be safe.' Then she said, 'The Armenians came down like a wolf on the fold,' and when I said that was the Assyrians, she said, 'Nonsense, dear, haven't you ever heard of the Armenian massacres?

They are a ruthless people.' He is to come on Friday, and now there is the formidable problem of whom to ask to make up our partie carrée. Aunt Lucy wants to ask Major Markette, a man who thinks that all students, workers, foreigners and women should be put under heavy restrictions, that all criminals should be kept in solitary confinement or executed and that all lunatics should be imprisoned for life; I cannot enjoy myself if he is in the same room, and what will Tigran Leontyev think? Armenians may be reactionary (are they like Poles or like Russians – I have never met one before) but I do not want to present him with Major Markette as a representative of English manhood. I am pressing the claims of a very quiet old portrait painter who never gets enough to eat and so is bound to accept the invitation. He may fall madly in love with Tigran Leontyev but at his age it surely will not matter, and in any case Aunt Lucy wouldn't notice. I will write and tell you how it goes off. It is nearly a week ahead, but already preoccupies most of our day. We have chosen the china, but not the menu; battle lines for timing have been drawn: the day before, I am to run round to Selfridges for the flowers (Moyses Stevens is nearer *and* dearer) and I am sure poor Mrs Lockett will have to resist strong pressure to start cooking the day before too. As for me, I am plotting how to smuggle in enough drink to float the evening off the ground. If it was my own party I should not have *begun* to think of any of these things; but you know how adaptable I am. I get into the spirit of Aunt Lucy's histrionics, and occasionally even enjoy them.

How is everything going with you? Do write and tell me about *your* party. You will look after Harvey for me, won't you? In spite of being so tall and authoritative, he is quite different inside.

I must go and read to Aunt Lucy. She has a passion for having things done for her that she could perfectly well do for herself.

Write to me –

Love, Cornelia

Mrs Bender to Harvey Lamb

Bede Street.
April 25th

My dear Harvey,

I am writing to tell you that Cornelia is well and happy – she is such a dear girl and I really believe that she enjoys the quiet life we live here and our little parties. I thought that perhaps you used to live at *rather* too fast a pace, and I think she agrees with me. I am sure this was the reason for the difficulties between you, which distress me so much – I pray for you every night, that this separation may end soon and things will be as they used to be. Cornelia is so fond of you, she speaks of you often and with great affection. She may be a little flighty, even frivolous, compared to you who are so steady, but she would never do anything wrong, and I am sure she is only longing to have you back and to do her part in putting things right.

I have not seen Hugo since Christmas – I had hoped he would come to me for Easter, but he says he is too busy. Of course he does far too much – at Christmas he would only take two days' rest, in spite of my pleading. I am afraid that as he gets older he is becoming very difficult and even quarrelsome. Your poor dear father would be very distressed to see it, we were all inseparable when we were children and he and Hugo were always such perfect friends. However, the fact that Hugo cannot come has enabled me to give Cornelia a home, and this I am very glad indeed to do.

I am enclosing a cutting of the poem Spencer had published in the *Reader's Digest*, isn't it charming? He is slowly but surely making a name for himself, in spite of the wretched critics who cannot bear anything that is *comprehensible*. He is getting on very well at his job at the Potato Board – isn't it strange to think of someone like him making his living at something so banal? But he is young. In time, as I tell him, he will take wing.

I hope you are having an interesting time in America – Cornelia tells me that in spite of everything you are enjoying your job. She says that in New York you live very well, though I do not know in what sense she can mean that – I am sure that amidst all the excitement and luxury you would be glad to come back to poor old England.

Cornelia is out at the moment, otherwise I should ask her to send a message. She is going to a great many galleries and exhibitions just now – I believe she feels that she must put this time with me to good use and improve her knowledge of things. *That* does not sound very frivolous, does it? Ah, Harvey, see that you don't misjudge her!

Bless you, my dear boy,

Your affectionate Aunt, Lucy

Mrs Nieman to Mrs Lamb New York.
May 1st

Dear Cornelia,

Thank you for your two letters. I have pleasure to report that Harvey came to dinner, that he got on well with Mel and that I like him very much. I invited the English girl from downstairs, I do not think he falls in love with her but she made a great fuss of him. Her face is slack, her teeth stick out, but she has a great energy and seems determined to make people take notice. She causes Mel pain, which he does not hide, but I had also General Carter and a very bien élevé couple from Massachusetts, and place the girl where Mel cannot see her, so he was not rude. They had an excellent dinner, naturally, and I think everybody amused themselves. Clive Carter and your Harvey find that they know some same people in London, so they are at ease, and apart from Prudence (that is the English girl – what a name!) thrusting herself between whenever they talk for long, I think he had a good time. He seems happy to come again although when I say drop in whenever you like he seems uncertain. I shall find him an apartment. He is rather formal when we talk of you and pretends nothing is wrong so I do the same. I find him très sympathique and I think he has a pleasant surprise to find that I am not beautiful in spite of being French.

How curious that you met Tigran. I knew he went to London but did not think him suitable to send to you. I suppose he will not be long in England. He has friends in Paris which is why he goes to Europe, to spend his vacation with them.

Mel sends his love,

Yours, Christiane

Mrs Lamb to Mrs Nieman Bede Street.
May 6th

Darling Christiane,

I have just come back from having a delicious dinner with Tigran and he said whenever I wrote to you I was to send you his love so I thought I'd do so immediately in case I forget. The only snag about this evening was that we were sitting in the Belle Meunière not doing a bit of harm when in walked the Home Secretary – you know he was at Oxford with Harvey and now, swinging on some *hinge of fate*, he is frightfully high on the poll for Prime Minister. We have kept up with them in a desultory way – I always thought he would be useful, but when I was trying to get someone out of Wormwood Scrubs he was *totally inert*. Anyway, he bent over our table and asked after Harvey, and Tigran insisted on leaping up and inviting him to join us. Somehow his accent sounded more stage Russian even than usual, and he had had rather a lot of brandy. Peter Bath looked very thoughtful and carefully produced his wife. If only he had had a bird with him we should have been quits! This is the second time I've met people I know in restaurants, Tigran is very impressed and says I know everybody but in fact it is extremely irritating because I don't want poor Harvey hearing all sorts of things that will worry him. When I went to Aunt Lucy's I didn't tell any of our friends where I was going. I thought I'd have a rest from all the good advice and commiseration *contingent*, as they say, on Harvey dashing off to N.Y. without me. However, I saw Margot the other day, and she asked me to a party, so if I go that will be the end of my invisibility. Even if I don't, she will tell all our friends where I am. We met *her* at the Empress, so I wonder where is safe? Tigran only wants to go to the Best Places – I have been toying with the idea of trying to pretend that Wimpy Bars are madly chic, of luring him into those places where the lighting makes the salad black, and telling him that all the people in there are terribly famous. If he was more interested in the arts it might work; or could I pretend they were all titled people down on their luck?

Our original dinner party – it seems quite a long time ago – was a great success although fraught, as usual, with possibilities of disaster. I managed to persuade Aunt L. that Major Markette would be a much less suitable choice than Roylance Cowlinshaw (the artist I told you about) – I said

Tigran was terribly interested in art – after all, isn't that how we met? – and would be thrilled to meet a real live artist. Poor old Roylance hasn't painted a picture for years, but Aunt Lucy likes to keep up the fantasy that whenever she sees him he is fresh from his atelier where some beauty has been posing in taffeta. He did once get into the Academy, and also did an enormous painting of Aunt Lucy in her riding-habit which used to hang in the hall in Gloucestershire and was imposed upon Uncle Hugo when she left the house. Now, poor old Roylance does occasional pastels of people's children and dogs; we simply do not know what he lives on. Aunt Lucy always says, Oh I think he's very comfortable, whenever the question of his extreme poverty comes up – she does not really believe in poverty, in the same way as a small child of our acquaintance once told us she did not believe in mice. The old boy was very impressed with Tigran as I thought he would be, and got very skittish towards the end of dinner. He had as much wine as I could smuggle through to him while Aunt Lucy was otherwise engaged, and talked at inordinate length about the Gang Show (which in case you don't know is a sort of revue performed entirely by Boy Scouts). Tigran was terribly baffled because before dinner Aunt Lucy had involved him in an extensive conversation about literature and one way and another I think he considers us an intellectual household. Roylance's ecstatic description of the can-can performed by twelve-year-old Wolf Cubs seemed to bewilder him completely, and Aunt Lucy was equally at a loss and tried to wrench the conversation in other directions (throwing several speaking looks at me, as though to say that Major Markette would never have been so tiresome). However, Roylance made up for it after dinner by being immensely gallant to Aunt Lucy, dancing attendance on her with the coffee-cups, the cigarette-box and the matches, and ending up sitting boyishly at her feet on a pouffe. Ah, said Aunt Lucy, you've chosen well, I always like a pouffe, they are so comfortable and friendly. I winked at Roylance, who let out a wild eldritch laugh. Aunt L. leaned over to Tigran and murmured that the poor old man had had too much to drink. (I know for a fact that he is exactly the same age as she is.) She said to me aside, '*Not* the port, I think,' in a satisfied stage-whisper; she always argues that alcohol is not necessary for social intercourse, even impedes it, and she likes to be proved right. In spite of these moments of tension, the evening could be counted a success, and Tigran was so good! He pretended to understand things that he didn't, and he ate everything, in spite of the fact that Aunt Lucy had instructed Mrs Lockett to cook the pods with the peas, producing a dish which I call *pois mange presque tout;* round everybody's plate there appeared little chewed balls of green thread, but not Tigran's; I do hope he has a good digestion. Everything else was in fact very nice though not abundant – I felt quite embarrassed looking at the size of Tigran's helping of pudding, considering his large frame. Since then, of course, I have seen him several times – three to be exact. He shows no signs of going to Paris. Christiane, *do* tell me about him – there are all sorts of things I dare*n't* ask in case he doesn't want to tell. I gather you met him when you were married to Adam. I said to him wittily, 'Ah, she knows you from Adam,' but he didn't understand the joke and had to have it explained. Considering he's only been speaking English (I gather) for about twelve years I think he speaks and understands marvellously – he seems to find an English accent very amusing, and well he might, when one comes to listen to oneself.

Thank you so much for your letter dear Christiane – I must finish this and go to bed. Aunt Lucy and I are going shopping tomorrow and I must get all the rest I can.

Yours ever, Cornelia

PS.—You are an angel to have Harvey to dinner, I'm so glad it was such a success.
PPS.—Do *do* write to me about Tigran!

Harvey Lamb to Mrs Bender New York.
May 7th

Dear Aunt Lucy,

Thank you so much for your letter of April 25th. I apologise for being so long in answering it, but I have a great deal of work to do here and have been forced to spend a good many evenings reading various despatches and telegrams. I am so glad to hear that Cornelia is settling down well and enjoying her stay with you. It is very good of you to have her. I would be most grateful if you would let me know from time to time how she is. I do not intend to write to her myself unless for some very important and specific purpose, because I want her to realise that the position between us is serious. I am afraid she is apt to think that any difficulties we may have can simply be glossed over and forgotten and that I do not mean it when I say that I cannot return to her unless she changes her attitude about certain subjects. I hope that when she has had time to think about things a little, she will see them as I do, but in the meantime, to write her friendly letters may make her feel that I am once again giving in to her, something I am determined not to do. I hope you do not think I am hard, especially when you have Cornelia with you, and can see that she is perhaps a little lonely and worried. But I am sure you agree with me that it is absolutely essential to be firm when dealing with someone like Cornelia, who sometimes seems determined not to take matters seriously. I rely on you, then, to keep me informed about her health and so on, because she is, in spite of everything, very dear to me.

The weather here is dreadfully hot and one longs for a cloudy English sky. Thank you so much for the cutting from the *Reader's Digest*. I am glad Spencer is making progress in his writing.

Please give my kind regards to Mrs Lockett, and to Uncle Hugo when next you see him.

Yours, Harvey

Mrs Nieman to Mrs Lamb

New York.
May 13th

Dear Cornelia,

I found an apartment for Harvey. It is very nice and not too far from his office, he can walk there in the mornings which will be good for his health. He already moved in and yesterday I helped him rearrange the furniture and make it look good. While we are doing this we have a long talk about you. He is sad but I think also rather determined. I do not think he repines for you so much that he will go back to you on any terms. I think you must take care. You would be very stupid to lose him, he is very nice, très sympathique, and making good money which I think certainly increases, in time. English people if good-looking are popular here and I think he soon gets friends and starts going to parties and perhaps learns to live without you. Prudence Darnley who lives in the apartment below us throws herself at him already without reservation. I try to conceal from her his new address, but he gives it to her as soon as she asks it of him, which I thought silly but too late to say so. He is not in danger from her but tout de même . . .

You ask me about Tigran. His mother was Polish, his father Armenian. They are both dead. He had a brother who disappeared sometime at the end of the war. He and Adam were friends from the Resistance Movement, they were in Warsaw together, then in England, then Paris and both came to America at the same time. I see Tigran quite often, he has a French fiancée at the moment and I am supposed to advice him how to handle her. He will visit her parents when he goes to Paris, they are extremely rich.

Mel sends his love.

Yours, Christiane

Mrs Lamb to Mrs Nash Bede Street.
May 17th

Darling Mary,

Isn't it awful the way the years go by and we never write to each other except for Christmas cards – I do hope you and the children and Larry are well. As you can see from the address I am staying temporarily with Harvey's Aunt Lucy – *he* has gone off to New York in a huff and I am left all alone in London to think things over, as Harvey says – he has been getting very fed up with me for a long time now and I can't say I really blame him. We gave up Edwardes Square when he was sent to New York and the idea is that at the end of the year we set up house again, I having reformed my character in the meantime. *You* know what chance there is of that, but still I don't see why it shouldn't work: it will give Harvey a chance to forget the more unpleasant things about me, at least that is what I hope. It is quite nice being here but there are complications and I am writing to ask whether you would be an angel and as it were underwrite me, if the occasion arises? I am quite certain it won't, but the thing is that I am going away on the 19th to spend a few days with some people of whom Aunt Lucy doesn't approve, and rather than have a long and tedious argument about it, I told her I was going to stay with you. She does tend to write to Harvey rather a lot, probably giving him progress reports on me, and she is so alarmist. She thinks these people are particularly fast, and would sow all sorts of seeds of doubt in poor Harvey's mind. I am confident that she will not actually check up on me, but knowing how things happen (do you remember the ghastly fiasco about you and Michael all those years ago?) I thought I would just warn you. I am sorry it is such short notice – but that would only matter if I was *really* coming to stay with you, wouldn't it?

Thank you so much, dear cousin – in haste,

Yours, Cornelia

Mrs Nash to Mrs Lamb

Everleigh,
Suffolk.
May 26th

Dear Cornelia,

I don't know why you put your request in the form of a question since you did not give me time to refuse. And I don't know why you say *people* of whom your Aunt Lucy and Harvey would not approve since it is clearly one person. I do think you might tell the truth to me at least, if to no one else.

It was nice to hear from you, all the same. I don't know what gave you the idea that we were all well – as I told you on my last Christmas card, Jeannie is pregnant and Larry broke his leg – but I suppose you could say that otherwise we are all right. Larry is in fact getting about again now, though he still limps. Jeannie is trying to make up her mind whether to get married. The other three are quite well, apart from worries about Christopher's O-levels and Elizabeth's teeth. I suppose all these things will sort themselves out somehow.

I am so sorry you and Harvey have parted. I hope it will be only for a short time. At least you have no children to complicate things. If you would like to come down and stay while you are on your own, we should love to see you. Larry and the children send their love.

Yours, Mary

Mrs Lamb to Mrs Nash

Bede Street.
May 28th

Darling Mary,

You are an angel to allow me to use you as an alibi – I am so grateful to you that I would do anything, simply anything, you asked me. Shall I come down and do the washing up for a week? I would send you huge bouquets if your garden was not already bursting with them. I was not being evasive when I said I was going to stay with people, rather than one person – I think I just wanted to spare you. This one person is an Armenian called Tigran Leontyev. I met him in the National Portrait Gallery and he is a friend of Christiane Perrier, that school friend of mine who married a man called Nieman and lives in New York. It strikes me as very strange that I went to the National Portrait Gallery specially to improve my mind, for Harvey, and *this* is the result, almost as though it had been a reward for my good intentions.

We stayed away for four days in a beam and horse-brass hotel in Wells which is one of the nicest towns I have ever been in. It rained a great deal, especially when we went to see dear Stonehenge. Tigran said they were like tame elephants, docile and yet with something left in them that man would never master, don't you think that intelligent? He is such a very large man, and I somehow find it easier to believe that small men are intelligent. Isn't it a wonderful name – I have always been so fond of lions and tigers. In fact, he is more like a large bear, very tall and broad. When I was a little girl I always thought how wonderful it would be if one had married some soppy prince, to wake up in the morning with a glorious bear.

Do write to me sometime. A millon thanks again.

Yours, Cornelia

I've just re-read your letter and darling I am so sorry about Larry's leg and Jeannie's baby. It seems unlikely that I could do anything to help, but if I could, do let me know.

Mrs Bender to Harvey Lamb Bede Street.
May 29th

My dear Harvey,

Thank you so much for your letter. I am glad to hear you are settling down as well as one could expect in a town which cannot be simpatico. Your dear father never thought highly of the Americans, and I do not suppose they have changed very much. I quite understand your decision not to write to Cornelia – the less she hears from you the more she will miss you. We are being cruel only to be kind! I will write once a month at least, to let you know how we are getting on, and to give you news of her.

She seems at the moment to be quite happy and is looking particularly well – she looked a little peaky when she first came to me, but the bloom has come back to her now that she has settled down. She does not seem to be seeing many of her old friends but perhaps it is all to the good that she has decided to live quietly while she is with me. The other evening she brought a foreign friend to dine – I believe he is Roumanian, but seemed extremely polite and well-informed. He was a friend of the French girl with whom Cornelia was at school, and was just passing through London on his way to Paris. Roylance came to make up the four and we had quite a merry evening. Roylance remarked how pretty Cornelia looked. He has the artist's discriminating eye.

There is just one thing that troubles me a little. Cornelia has been to spend a few days with her cousin Mary in Suffolk, and when she returned, although she looked very well and seemed to have enjoyed herself, she had several very large bruises on her arm. When I asked what she had done, she seemed not to want to talk about it; she said she had fallen out of a tree. I wanted to put something on it, but she would not let me look at it closely. I do not know why, but I felt she was not telling the truth, and I could not help thinking about Larry Nash. You know what a peculiar man he is, he drinks and his language is sometimes dreadful, I shall never forget him at Humphrey's wedding. I could not help wondering whether perhaps she had had some sort of unpleasant scene with him – I believe he is sometimes quite violent. I do not want to alarm you, but I am a little worried about it, especially as she said she might be going down again later on in the summer. Of course she could not come to any real harm, but nevertheless one does not like to think of that kind of thing.

Cornelia has just come in, and asks me to send you her love. She is going off to the National Portrait Gallery again today. She seems to find it extremely interesting. I must go with her one of these mornings, I have not been in it since I was a girl.

Bless you my dear boy. Do write to me and let me know

all your doings, and trust me to write to you, in my capacity as duenna!

Your loving aunt, Lucy

Mrs Lamb to Harvey Lamb

Bede Street.
May 29th

Darling darling Har-har!

How are you, how is New York, are you having a lovely time? Life at Aunt Lucy's is really very pleasant, although at this moment it is enshrouded in a very black cloud because last night we had a Poetry Reading and Spencer brought a *girl*! More consternation could not have been caused if he had entered leading an ostrich. She was called Linda and was wearing boots, which Aunt Lucy pressed her to take off in the hall. 'I could lend you some slippers, dear,' she said, 'although . . . ' and she looked from her own feet to poor Linda's which were three sizes larger. Linda refused the kind offer and I am not surprised – the boots looked as if they would have to be *cut* off – and Aunt Lucy then passed to various other items such as her jacket and the shoulder-bag she was carrying and tried to part her from these. Aunt Lucy is the only woman in London who can make one feel that the only reason for not taking off one's jacket is that one's blouse is dirty. The wretched girl managed to keep all her clothes and sat down by Spencer, who basely refused to defend her. We all sipped our sherry, the poets shuffled their papers, and Aunt Lucy remarked to me sotto voce that 'the poor girl was suffering from that dreadful disease Dr Dench was telling me about, it causes dark marks around the eyes.' Did I ever tell you about Fishtoft, the new poet? He was the disruptive element last time because he ate too much and would not be pleasant. He was not here last night and neither was the boy who

Mrs Lockett and I have wittily christened Spencer's fairy queen. *He* must have been replaced by Linda; perhaps a volcanic change is taking place inside dear Spencer. Aunt Lucy has taken up again the idea that he should put an 's' in his name instead of a 'c' because she says she is sure he is related to the original one. She commissioned me to look for him in the National Portrait Gallery, to prove a likeness (I haven't found him yet). Personally, Spencer reminds me more of the vest than the poet. He read something last night which plumbed the saltless depths of bathos and was roundly applauded for it. Nevertheless, Linda was a considerable blot on his copybook, and darkened the evening: as soon as they had all gone Aunt Lucy began talking about Ingratitude and then scolded Mrs Lockett for not understanding some ambiguous point about the sandwiches. I did not escape: Aunt Lucy's advice to me was to use less perfume. She said it made her feel faint and reminded her of a cheap woman who had once tried to get Uncle Hugo. I thought it an odd adjective considering that I was wearing a Dior at six guineas half a fluid ounce, but as Aunt Lucy herself would say, No matter! Tomorrow Poor Maud is coming to tea, perhaps that will cheer her up.

As you can see, je m'amuse. It is glorious weather here though a week ago, when I was in the country, it rained and rained. I hope it is not too hot in New York, I hope you are having a wonderful time. Christiane *loves* you, isn't that nice? She tells me all sorts of nice things about you and says there is an English lady madly in love with you in the basement!

I am going to run out now and post this letter and buy Aunt Lucy some anemones – Neville's Favourite Flower!

Lots of love, Cornelia

Mrs Lamb to Mrs Nieman Bede Street.
May 29th

Dearest Christiane,

What an angel you are to find a flat for Harvey, to help him with his furniture, to talk to him and defend him from this Prudence. As to the last, I hope you will not be *too* assiduous – dear Har does deserve a little fling, and it would surely be more dangerous if she were a raving beauty? But I leave it all to you – you are a wise, kind girl and if Harvey is not in love with *you* by now, he is very undiscriminating.

I have just been writing to my cousin Mary – do you remember her, a tall, dark, good-looking girl who has now, however, gone to seed in Suffolk. She is in fact extremely kind and amiably allowed me to use her as an alibi when I went off for a few days with Tigran. But she is also severe; I have just been writing to her, to thank her, and finding it rather hard, because all the time I could hear her carping, between the lines.

I came back from the country tottering, but I don't think Aunt Lucy noticed. When you have spent four days of unmitigated pleasure it is difficult to behave rationally at the end of it; I never was more grateful for Aunt L.'s myopia. Yesterday, when reading to her from a particularly repellent historical novel of the odds bodikins variety, I suddenly started to cry and had to begin coughing instead; only hours before I had had to use the same disguise for a sort of idiot laughter. Now Aunt L. thinks my lungs are, as she puts it, 'affected' and wants me to see Doctor Dench. My euphoria is mixed with an immense impatience which is not a good mood in which to read about wimples and stomachers throughout the hours of a summer afternoon. Tigran's vacation will be finished soon. We meet almost every day in the

National Portrait Gallery in front of Landseer in his studio. We have given up trying to find restaurants where we won't meet people; the only place which proved absolutely safe was the greyhound track, but he *would* bet and although he says he is 'verry rrich' (is he?) I decided that privacy was too expensive. Now we sit smouldering in places like the Jardin des Gourmets, or Alberts where it's dark. At least *I* smoulder – the scent he uses has the most frightful effect on me, I am simply seething by the end of dinner and then of course there is Nowhere to Go. He is staying with his uncle and aunt, people of monumental respectability. They do not like him to stay out late, or get drunk; they want him to spend his evenings with them at the Polish Hearth. I think they are unreasonable, but he says they are old and sad. I ask why he doesn't move out into a hotel and he says he couldn't do that. I am very much alarmed at how much I like him, quite apart from anything else. He is so cheerful and so kind. Aunt Lucy suddenly remembered him the other day. She asked me whether my Roumanian friend would like to come to one of our poets' evenings. I said he had left London. I daren't ask him here again. I keep seeing letters to Harvey in the hall; and even if she didn't suspect anything *he* might. Besides, being in that shaded room with all those big sofas woud be more than I could bear.

I shall have to stop soon as we are expecting Poor Maud – a lady whose main claim to fame is that she once sued *The Times* for a misprint: they referred to her husband as 'the well-known baker' when in fact he was something very important in the Big Five. Since then she has been hounded, in a small way, by misfortune – a natural effect, I should have thought, of opposing the voice of Jove. She always has some new disaster to tell, and those disasters recall others, most of which have a patina of age and repetition but are none the less enjoyable for that. Aunt Lucy has her own collection, specialising in cruel husbands and ungrateful servants. Poor Maud's stories are about inaccurate doctors and dreadful accidents. When she has gone, Aunt Lucy and I will sit down and welter in our comfort, like people returning to a warm fireside after seeing a film about disastrous arctic explorations.

Mrs Lockett has just knocked on my door: the festivities have begun. Please give my love to Melville and to Harvey when next you see him.

Yours, Cornelia

Mrs Nieman to Mrs Lamb New York.
June 4th

Dear Cornelia,

I am amazed to hear that Tigran stays in London when he is all the time expected in Paris. Angélique Mouscadet, his fiancée, telephoned her parents to ask what they think of him, and heard that he has not arrived. I do not think you are doing a good thing, to keep him in London. You spoil his chances of marrying in a very wealthy family, which would be quite the best thing for him. He is not so young, and he will ruin his health if he goes on dissipating as he does at the moment. I am trying to reassure Angélique, but it is not easy. She tells me yesterday she is sure he has found some woman in London, and she is angry. I do my best but she is not patient. He does not write to her, only a postcard from some country place. She telephones me, very upset, and says he has sent her a picture of gravestones. Besides this, there is the question of Harvey. You said yourself he may find out, and if he did, that is the end. He is doing very well here, everybody likes him and he has a good career. He is really too good for a flirt like you and you ought to realise it and not put your whole marriage in danger. You say something about Tigran being rich – he is not. He makes very good money but never saved a centime of it. What he does not spend on himself and women he gives to people who do not deserve it. Many people wished to marry him but it would be no sense to marry someone poor. He is too extravagant. I warn you, Cornelia, not to delude yourself.

Yours, Christiane

Mrs Lamb to Mrs Nieman Bede Street.
June 9th

Darling Christiane don't be so French! Why do you think of everything in terms of money? I haven't the slightest intention of marrying Tigran if that is what you mean in telling me not to delude myself. And I really don't think he needs to look for an heiress for his old age just yet; your description of him as 'not so young' and dissipated to boot, sounds like the famous statistician's paper on 'the British population broken down by age and sex.' He is not particularly broken down and besides he is extremely fond of Angélique. He says she is a sweet girl. Only the other day I went with him to Harrods where he bought her an extremely expensive blouse. I feel a great affection for the girl, and I spent a lot of time on that blouse. It was altogether a very successful trip to Harrods – Tigran caused a sensation by kissing me in the food department, where he bought some Polish sausage for Mrs Woronowski and some peaches in brandy for Aunt Lucy. I told him that I did not want to remind her of his existence and that the peaches would be put in the larder for a special occasion there to be found after her death; but it is not possible to stop him from doing something that he wants to.

I don't see why it is so important for him to go to Paris – surely he does not have to ask for her hand? I am not at all sure, in any case, that Angélique is the right girl for him. She sounds as though she has a suspicious nature, and her bosom, Tigran told me while we were choosing the blouse, is 'razzer sin'. (Isn't his voice extraordinary? I have never liked my name so much as when it is pronounced Corr-nellyah.) I am not at all sure that it is any longer a sensible thing to do, for a man to marry a rich woman. It was all very well once, when a woman, however rich, could be kept in her place.

As for Harvey, you are quite right, of course he is too good for me, that has been the trouble all along. I have given up hope that he may ever slip, even a little, and I don't seem to be able to be any better. But with all his virtues I love him still and I *think* he loves me. So there is no need to worry. The pattern you have ordained for us all will be adhered to, you are keeping the threads together at your end, and though a little unravelling may be going on here, it can all be knitted up again.

Yours affectionately, Cornelia

Mrs Lamb to Mrs Nieman

Hotel de Lys,
Paris.
June 15th

Darling Christiane,

You will be glad to hear that Tigran is doing his duty: at this very moment he is making himself agreeable in the salon of the Mouscadets. I don't suppose you will give me any credit for it, but it was really I who persuaded him. I told him you were worried, I even sketched for him your vision of his impecunious dotage. He laughed and said you were a wonderful person. Then he said 'Okay, let's go to

Paris tomorrow.' One of the things I love about him is that he is so *obedient*. So here I am, in a little sitting-room with cupids on the ceiling. The curtains are open so that I can see the dark blue night sky flooded with that peculiar pink light, and hear the sound of whistles being blown and tyres whiffling and the roaring sound of the traffic on the boulevard. We only arrived at midday, but already Tigran has logged several hours with the Mouscadets. He went round there this afternoon, and was invited back for supper. During the three hours between his coming back and going out again he several times announced that he was going to cry off the dinner, but I insisted. He is very much impressed with the Mouscadets' house. It has a courtyard, butlers, statues, wrought iron gates *inside*, and, he said, a fashionable type of dog. His in-laws-to-be were somewhat formidable, but they could not resist him for long. He said complacently that they liked him *very* much. I sent him off half an hour ago in his grey silk suit, carrying a bunch of roses for Madame. I have become such a partisan for your plans that I had a genuine pang of alarm when he said that there was, beside the statues and menservants, a *beautiful* maid. I know there is a sort of traditional droit de seigneur in some of these families, but I think it is a little early for him to start.

As for me, I have had a quiet afternoon, except for one extraordinary encounter: I met M. Bellavance, the man on the boat! I went out for a walk, bought a bunch of daisies and cornflowers, and then found myself at the corner of a street whose name seemed to mean something to me – and then I remembered M. Bellavance, in a throbbing cabin in the crew's quarters, telling me where he lived. Naturally, I turned down the street, just out of respect for his memory, and then suddenly saw him coming towards me. We talked very amiably. He said, 'You are living in Paris?', looking at my bouquet, and I think he was relieved when I said no. He kept glancing at his house, a few steps away, and at last asked me in. I had detected in him for some seconds the usual signs of masculine calculation about the possible consequences of invitations like this, and had decided virtuously to refuse. I think he was perhaps a little relieved at that too – he seemed younger even than I remembered him. But he insisted that we exchange addresses, and suddenly starting to talk French, said that if I was in Paris the following week perhaps we could meet then. It struck me at first that he might have forgotten who I was, or confused me with someone else he had met in the same circumstances, of whom there must be many, if he travels at all widely – he always seemed to me a young man who makes hay even when it is raining. But at the end he formally gave me good wishes from his brother François. Chez François was where we used to meet on the ship. He walked with me to the corner and seemed quite sorry to part from me, and so should I have been if I had not been coming back here.

Now I am safe back in our hotel room, which I shan't leave again, except to go downstairs and dine. I had thought of going out tonight, perhaps ringing up the Labour Attaché, who is an old friend of Harvey's, but I have decided not to – I want to be here in case Tigran gets back early from the Mouscadets. I have unpacked, arranged the flowers and looked several times out of the windows and into all the mirrors – there are four in this room and three in the other one. The wallpaper is made to look like quilted satin, blue with pink bows, and seems to me to be extremely pretty. I am writing this on the table, which has actually got a heavy cover with a pile so thick that it pricks my arms, and I have spread Tigran's silk scarf to protect myself. This must be the only hotel in Paris which hasn't gone over to square blond furniture with stainless steel corners.

I had a certain amount of difficulty getting away from Aunt Lucy. I simply had to use poor Mary again, in spite of her disapproval. I said that Mary was ill and had no one to look after her—her husband has broken his leg, so it sounded reasonable. Aunt Lucy at once suggested ringing up the agency where she got Mrs Lockett (last of the line of saints and martyrs) and having somebody sent down to help Mary. I told her they would not be able to afford that, which diverted her on to the subject of Larry, who is one of her favourite examples of cruel husbands married to admirable, long-suffering wives. He is a sculptor, which Aunt Lucy would consider very romantic if he was not married. I hope I did convince her, because if she has any suspicions at all she has only to look into my wardrobe to have them confirmed. I could not possibly defend the necessity of taking my black moiré trouser suit, or even my Mary Quant Lace, to Suffolk. I promised not to be away very long and to telephone her when I was coming back, a chore I am afraid poor Mary will have to look after. Aunt L. was very put out and after her first expressions of sympathy began to feel that Mary's suffering did not excuse her selfishness in asking me to attend to her when I ought to be reading to Aunt Lucy. But my sense of responsibility is wearing thin. I am beginning to feel that all these camouflages are unnecessary, and in fact from the moment I looked out my passport, there has been a distinct smell of burning boats. But don't be afraid. Tigran must fly back to America in a fortnight, and surely nothing irreversible can happen in that time.

Don't be cross with me!

Yours, Cornelia

Mrs Lamb to Mrs Nash

Hotel de Lys,
Paris.
June 15th

Darling Mary,

I do hope you will not mind that I have used you again; but I promise it is for the very last time. I came here at twenty-four hours' notice – a fact which would have shocked poor Aunt Lucy almost as much as my coming here at all. She thinks foreign travel should be approached with ceremony and that several days should be spent in rituals involving lists, fresh tissue paper, keys, labels, and conversations with airports, stations and taxi ranks. Perhaps this would not be her *main* objection in my case, but it would be a double shock, and after all she is 75. So I told her you were ill, and that poor Larry, with his broken leg (a nice titbit of truth) couldn't do very much, and I was going down for a few days until you could get someone to help. I promised to let her know when I was coming back, so could you be a very kind girl and telephone her about the 20th and tell her I'll be back very soon. It will please her, and reassure her as well. She was so querulous about *when* you rang up (just when she had gone to sleep) and *how* you rang up (you sent one of the children to the farm) that I thought for a moment that she doubted me. So a phone call from you would be just what she needs.

We have only been here for half a day. Tigran has been out for most of the time so I have had plenty of leisure to write letters. It is hot here, but it looks beautiful and nobody is throwing stones. I am sitting by a window looking at a plane-tree and as you can see running out of things to write. So I will end by sending you my love and my undying gratitude – I think we will be here just long enough for you to reply, which I should like *very* much.

Yours ever, Cornelia

Mrs Nash to Mrs Lamb June 20th

Dear Cornelia,

As before, I am in no position to refuse to help you, but I must say I think you are being very silly. However short-sighted your Aunt Lucy may be, there will surely be something to give you away, and I don't think she will take kindly to the fact that you have been diddling her and her favourite nephew on quite so grand a scale. Incidentally, I have no intention of telephoning her to say when you will be back. If I am forced to lie for you I will do so, but I am not going to take such a deliberate risk. You had better telephone her from the airport if you want to warn her of your return.

Later.

I had to break off, and couldn't finish this letter till today, although there is nothing much else to say. I am sorry if I sound rather cross – it has always irritated me that you look so harmless and well behaved, and yet always get away with things. As you reminded me, the only time I tried anything of the sort, it ended in a disastrous muddle. Incidentally, I saw Michael the other day – he is a farmer, with a wife and three children.

Let me know when you are back in England. I might possibly be able to get away for a few days in London sometime this year. I can't afford it, but I feel that if I spend any longer in this sort of life without a break, I shall become a complete bumpkin.

Yours, Mary

Sir Hugo to Mrs Bender *Pigpound Lane.*
June 22nd

Dear Lucy,

I am proposing to come to London by the 4.10 on Friday and hope to go on the following day to Zambia. I may look in at the Botanical Conference if I have time.

Yours, Hugo

Mrs Bender to Sir Hugo Lamb Bede Street.
June 24th

Dear Hugo,

Thank you so much for letting me know that you are coming to London – perhaps you could dine with us one evening while you are here? I know Cornelia would love to see you. She is away just at the moment, but only for a few days. Do telephone me when you are settled in, but give us just a little notice – you know what Mrs Lockett is!

I have a flourishing exchange with Harvey – he is such a good correspondent. You will be glad to know that he is getting on excellently with his work in spite of having to live among those dreadful people – if only poor Geoffrey could have lived to see the success he has made! I saw poor Maud the other day and we were talking of old times. She sent you her love and said what a long time it was since she had seen you. She wondered that you were so seldom in London – I told her that, as Mrs Lockett would say, it was not for want of asking!

Please excuse this short letter – Mrs Lockett is standing by waiting for the post.

Your affectionate sister, Lucia

Mrs Lamb to Mrs Nieman

Wood Cottage,
Pigpound Lane,
Pott Shrigley,
Cheshire.
June 24th

Darling Christiane,

I have put the address at the top of this letter not because I expect you to reply to me here (I am not sure how long we will be able to stay) but because it is such a lovely address. In case you didn't know it, Pott Shrigley is one of the prettiest places in the world, though I am sure that is not why Uncle Hugo chose it. It is much more likely to be because it is near to some particular bog where something special grows. Uncle Hugo has lived in this cottage for thirty-seven years without moving or changing anything so that the curtains and furniture seem to grow in their places; the ceilings and lintels are low, as though the cottage was sinking into the ground. The garden is grassy right up to the walls, ivy is coming in at the windows. There is a special pair of scissors on the bathroom window-sill, for cutting off the shoots. There are several rooms, but only two of them seem to be used. The rest are repositories for the various phases of Uncle Hugo's existence before he became a plant explorer, mouseoleums as Mrs Locket would say, for the separate causes to which he has been wedded, in his time. They are full of cricket bats, rocks, books, vast piles of paper (he once started a new translation of the Koran), statues and mysterious pieces of wood. The one usable bedroom has a vast brass bedstead but is almost entirely dark, because of the ivy. The living-room downstairs has bigger windows but they have Archbishop of Canterbury eyebrows of rambler roses which filter the light. The chairs have sagged so much that one's posture in them is as though one were sitting on the very latest from Conrans, but more comfortable; the pattern on the chintz is just discernible, the stamens of the cabbage roses making little dots like Cheshire cat grins now that the petals have disappeared. It is clean because Uncle Hugo, incredible as it may seem, was once in the Navy; he has lived through innumerable wars, so I suppose he had to be in something. The kitchen is very tidy, in a Tiggy-Winkle kind of way, so much so that I would have feared a Daily if I had not remembered Uncle Hugo's decided, though somewhat inconsistent, opinions about women. 'They are the very devil once you get them inside a house,' I heard him say once, which made me feel as though we were those 'sleek and shining creatures of the chase' which Tennyson rather unpleasantly remarked that men hunted for the beauty of their skins.

Perhaps I should tell you how we got here. We only stayed a short time in Paris. Tigran thought that three visits was quite enough to endear himself for life to the Mouscadets. He really was very good, Christiane, and I hope you are pleased with him because he endured two dinners and one luncheon, and although he was very kind about them they were clearly ineffable bores. The food was superb but the conversation was entirely about money and royalty. As his mission was completed I thought perhaps we ought to get back in case Aunt Lucy started to fret, especially as I had a scolding letter from Mary Nash refusing to telephone to Bede Street as I had asked her to do. I telephoned myself, dutifully, as soon as we got to the airport, only to be told a tale of woe by Mrs Lockett: Sir Hugo had arrived, without so much as a by-your-leave, and moved in lock stock and barrel and Mrs Bender was so angry that for a little while she seemed almost compos mentis: a sad state for poor Aunt Lucy to be in! Uncle

Hugo, it transpired, is on his way to Zambia on a plant-exploring expedition. While Mrs Lockett was talking – she has an elliptical style which gives one plenty of time for thought – I had this brilliant inspiration. I told her to tell Aunt Lucy I had rung up from Mary's to say I would be away for another week or so. And now here we are in Pigpound Lane! I am not sure how Tigran is going to take to country life; he has already proposed that we should go to a roadhouse tomorrow night, and Uncle Hugo's old radio has been wheezing away all day. He is getting through the readable books at rather an alarming rate. There are not many of them and in any case he is not what one would call the studious type. However we did find, between Gibbon and Ruskin, a copy of the Kama Sutra with certain passages marked, and with dates attached, one of which was 1902, which makes you think.

We have promised ourselves a trip to Manchester, but I am not sure whether this will satisfy Tigran's thirst for gaiety, or his desire to spend immense amounts of money on food and drink. He has arranged to hire a car, and he says he is going to get a portable television set, which will at least partially assuage his insatiable generosity. But though at this moment he is lying on his back under the apple-tree and actually chewing a grass stalk, he has only been there five minutes, and that is about his limit for such rural inactivities. He will jump up and come in and start cooking the dinner much too early. He is a brilliant cook, he tells me, and I believe him.

This pattern of life, which seems to me entirely delightful, may not appeal to him for long; on the other hand, the alternative is Uncle Woronowski and the Polish Hearth, and good-bye to the brass bedstead. Whatever we do, we have only got ten days left. At the end of that we shall all go back to our places in the scheme of things; order will be restored. You will be able to plan a prosperous future for Tigran and Angélique and for Harvey and me, and Mary Nash will have no more need to scold me. I leave you to contemplate that pleasant prospect, while I look out of the window.

Tigran sends his love.

Yours, Cornelia

Mrs Lamb to Mrs Nash

Wood Cottage,
Pigpound Lane,
Pot Shrigley.
June 23rd

Dearest Mary,

We have just moved here from Paris, so I thought I ought to write to you immediately, to let you know where I am. I am going back to London in just over a week, so after this I promise I shall not ask you for any more help. It did not matter a bit that you didn't telephone Aunt Lucy –I did so myself, and discovered that this cottage was empty, which seemed too good an opportunity to miss, so I am staying with you a few days longer, I hope you don't mind.

This is a remote place hidden from the road; so far nobody has even noticed that we are here. We are buying our groceries from the next village, so that there won't be talk. I suppose someone is bound to notice us soon – Tigran is not the sort of person one could hide for long – but I don't think Uncle Hugo would be upset unduly. He has gone to Zambia to look at some lilies, and provided he gets there while they are still in flower, he will be in a mellow mood when he gets back. We have not done any harm, except for breaking one small window-pane, which we had to do to get in. The cottage is enclosed, like a witch-ball in a net, with a web of ivy, jasmine and roses, so that the broken pane doesn't show and won't let the rain in. There are some pieces of glass in the garden shed, so we shall be able to repair the damage before we go.

Tigran wants to know who I am writing to. I told him a very sweet and charming woman, so he sends his love.

Yours, Cornelia

Mrs Nash to Mrs Lamb June 25th

Dear Cornelia,

Thank God I've found you – I was about to throw the whole stupid business up and tell your Aunt Lucy the truth. I have had a telegram from her, or rather you have, reading simply: 'Come back at once.' Your letter arrived just as I was going up to the farm to telephone. I suppose you will be going straight back to London, which is just as well, as I should think nothing but trouble could come of your breaking into somebody else's house and living there without their permission. You are mad if you think you can live in a village anywhere for forty-eight hours without anyone knowing, let alone a week. However, this is your business. If you leave now, perhaps you will get away with it again.

I hope your aunt is not seriously ill. I suppose she will wonder what has happened when she does not get a reply to her wire. If I get any more, I propose to ignore them. You will have to think of some reason why you did not respond sooner.

I am writing to you, rather than telegraphing, because I thought the delivery of a telegram would be more likely to draw attention to you than a letter.

Yours, Mary

Mrs Lamb to Mrs Nash

Bede Street.
June 28th

Darling Mary,

All is well! I dashed down here immediately I got your letter, leaving Tigran in the cottage, because I intend to go back there the day after tomorrow. I told Aunt Lucy her telegram had been delayed, blaming the Post Office, for whose inefficiencies one cannot be too grateful at times like these. I told her I had to get back to you, just till the end of the week, when someone else was coming to take my place. She is using all her most complicated mechanisms of disapproval and persuasion on me, but I am quite impervious. I am going to borrow Margot's car to drive up, and shall bring Tigran back next Friday, in time to catch his plane.

Aunt Lucy is not ill, but she is having trouble with Uncle Hugo, whose journey to Zambia has been delayed, so he is, as she puts it, lolling about here, disrupting the household. I never knew anyone who lolled less than Uncle Hugo, but it is one of Aunt Lucy's most pejorative words and she uses it somewhat indiscriminately. She does not so much want him to go, as to feel that he should, and for this my presence is necessary. She treats Mrs Lockett with inordinate solicitude whenever he is within earshot and constantly bewails the burden of work entailed by having two guests in the house. In this she gets no support from Mrs Lockett, nor from me. After all, Aunt Lucy has interrupted my holiday and I don't see why I should exert myself to make Uncle Hugo uncomfortable. So I have volunteered to do any extra work there is, while I am here, which cannot be much as he eats almost nothing and never has a bath. Aunt Lucy is very cross, and her manner towards me is pinched and distant. When we are alone she makes remarks, apparently to a third party, about how little some people think about the comfort and convenience of others. I am taking advantage of her displeasure to retire to my little room and write to you. There is an hour to go before dinner. Uncle Hugo has gone to the airways office again and Aunt Lucy is lying on the sofa in the drawing-room from which she makes occasional forays into the kitchen to see how Mrs Lockett is struggling with the burden of another mouth to feed. From a position of complete ignorance she will be giving all sorts of advice. It is what I call pressure cooking and does not noticeably improve the food. Perhaps she is dropping a little something extra into Uncle Hugo's share.

I suppose I ought to be depressed by the peculiar character of these Lambs, which, after all, Harvey may have inherited. But I imagine 'poor Geoffrey', Harvey's father, had the peculiarities in a less concentrated form. He must have been less intelligent than Uncle Hugo, less domineering than Aunt Lucy and less selfish than both; or so he looks in his photograph, which Aunt Lucy has kindly put in my bedroom, in a silver frame. Their energetic longevity, if inheritable, is certainly cheering, even though Aunt Lucy has never used hers for anything but furiously driving little social and emotional wheels. Poor Geoffrey does not look as though he had the astonishing reserves of animosity which seem to do them so much good; perhaps he died sooner because he was nicer.

Mrs Lockett has just been in with the message that if I could possibly spare a few minutes Mrs Bender would like to see me in the drawing-room. Mrs L.'s funny little spoon-face had that suppressed air which she always wears when there is trouble. I don't know whether to expect sherry or some enigmatically worded reproach. Either way I must end; however unwelcome my presence in the drawing-room

I am almost sure Aunt Lucy will not let me go again. I have been here half an hour – about the limit of endurance for being alone.

Thank you, dear cousin, for everything.

Yours, Cornelia

Tigran Leontyev to Mrs Lamb

Darling Cornelia,

I write this hasty note hoping you find it when you come. Just after you left a man came to cottage, looked through window and went away. Then two policemen came and asked me what I do here. I said nothing, not to get you in trouble, so they ask me to go with them. I do not know where. They are both tall and thin and I could have clouted them if I wish but thought better not. I will telephone you when I can.

Love and kisses, Tigran

Mrs Lamb to the Rt. Hon. Peter Bath

27 Bede Street,
W.1.
June 29th

Dear Peter,

Could you please help me? A friend of mine is in trouble with the police, but he has done absolutely *nothing wrong*, so obviously a mistake has been made, which I am sure you could put right by a stroke of the pen. His name is Tigran Leontyev and he was staying in a cottage at Pott Shrigley belonging to my Uncle (Sir Hugo Lamb). He was alone there when some policemen came and took him away, but I do not know where he is at the moment and it is very important that he should be released by next Friday, as he is due to go back to America. I am afraid he will lose his job if he is late, so I wonder whether you could look into this very quickly. I am so sorry to bother you, but as Harvey is in New York I have no one to help me and I thought you were the best person to write to.

Please give my love to Diana, I do hope we shall all meet soon.

Yours, Cornelia

I tried to telephone you but your office asked me to write.

Mr Rawsthorne to Mrs Lamb Home Office.

July 1st

Dear Madam,

As the Home Secretary is away from the office for a few days I am replying to your letter of the 29th.

I have been in touch with the Cheshire police and they inform me that the case of Mr Tigran Leontyev has been remanded for a week while further enquiries are made. I am afraid this is all the information I can give you at the moment, but I have requested the Chief Constable to communicate with me as soon as any further developments occur, when I will get in touch with you again.

I am, Madam,

Your obedient servant, E. Rawsthorne

Memo from Mr Rawsthorn to Mr Bath
Home Secretary

I thought you ought to see this letter from Mrs Lamb, and my reply. I append the report of the Cheshire police, as I thought you would want to deal with this personally on your return, particularly in view of the recent events at Crufty.

E. Rawsthorne

Report of Sergeant Brothers,
Pott Shrigley Police Station

At 4.15 on the 27th inst. I received a call at the Station from Colonel Sapling, who informed me that an unknown stranger had been seen in Sir Hugo Lamb's cottage in Pigpound Lane. Colonel Sapling told me that Sir Hugo was abroad, and that he had specifically informed Colonel Sapling that during his absence the cottage would be empty, as he did not desire to let it or lend it to anyone. Accordingly I went with P.C. Trew to the address, Wood Cottage, Pigpound Lane where I saw Tigran Leontyev. I asked him whether he had Sir Hugo Lamb's permission to be in residence there. He informed me of his name, and that he was an American citizen, but beyond that he would say nothing. As he could not furnish any reason for his presence there, I asked him to accompany me to the station. On returning to the cottage P.C. Trew discovered that it had been entered by force, a window in the kitchen having been broken. He also discovered ladies' clothing in the cupboards, but when questioned about this Leontyev again refused to say anything. I accordingly decided to keep him in custody on a charge of breaking and entering. He appears to have very little money and could not suggest any person who could furnish bail.

Mrs Lamb to Harvey Lamb Bede Street.
July 3rd

Darling Harvey,

I do hope this letter will not be too much of a shock to you but the truth is that I am in a mess and I very much need your help. It is rather urgent and I would have liked to telephone you only I didn't know your number and in any case it is such a complicated story that I don't think it would tell very well over the telephone, especially at such expense.

A little while ago I met a friend of Christiane's, an Armenian called Tigran Leontyev. I saw him a few times and then he went to Paris. When he got back he still had about a week of his holiday left and nowhere to spend it so I suggested he might borrow Wood Cottage, as Uncle Hugo was here in London on his way to Zambia. Almost the first thing that happened to the poor man when he got to Pott Shrigley was that two policemen came and arrested him, I cannot imagine why, and they are keeping him in prison. He is due back in America in a few days and I am afraid he will lose his job if he doesn't get back in time. I wrote at once to Peter Bath, but all I got back was a letter from some quite different person, an obedient servant, saying that Tigran had been remanded for a week.

Now something even more worrying has happened. Today in the papers there is a story of the theft of seven hundred and fifty guinea-pigs from a place called Crufty Research Centre, and the article goes on: 'A man of Russian extraction who was found in an uninhabited cottage at the near-by village of Pott Shrigley is being held for questioning.' As though Tigran had something to do with it! Darling Harvey, an awful miscarriage of justice is going on and we simply must do something about it. Tigran would not go about stealing guinea-pigs. You can check with Christiane about him – he is a very respectable man, and was a hero of the resistance movement in Poland and other places during the war. He is a very old and trusted friend of Christiane's first husband and she has known him for a long time. Do you think you could telephone to Peter Bath and explain that Tigran is a friend of ours – it would make it sound better if you said you know him – and ask him to do something? I have telephoned him myself today but he was extremely evasive and pretended that there was nothing he could do until the investigations had been completed. He seemed to be more concerned with trying to trace Uncle Hugo in Zambia than anything else, which is ridiculous, considering that he is not there. In fact he is here, in the next room. (His flight to Zambia has been delayed.) I didn't tell Peter this. Perhaps I should have done, but I thought it would just make it all more complicated if they were to drag Uncle Hugo in.

Darling, you will help, won't you? Would you telephone me after you have spoken to Peter Bath and let me know how you got on, and whether there is anything more I can do? Of course if you could come over it would be even better, I'm sure we could get it all straightened out – you have so many strings you could pull – isn't Charles Dawtry a Permanent Secretary somewhere now? And there's the Moxons and all sorts of people; and besides, it would be so nice to see you!

I will get this posted at once and wait impatiently and anxiously to hear from you.

All my love, Cornelia

Mrs Lamb to Mrs Nieman Bede Street. July 3rd

Darling Christiane,

The most appalling things are happening here – Tigran is in prison! It is only partly my fault, but I am terribly worried about it as I do not know where he is or for how long they will keep him. I have just written to Harvey to ask him to help; will you back me up? I told him that

Tigran was a very respectable person who would not do anything against the law, that you had known him for years etc. and I think I gave the impression that he was rather *old*. So when Harvey mentions it, you will give Tigran a good character, won't you?

It all happened because of our going to that cottage of Uncle Hugo's where we were having a heavenly time until I was summoned back to London by Aunt Lucy. I went for one night, to please her, and when I got back to the cottage again Tigran was not there. I found a note under the pillow – I can't think how he can have written it with the house full of policemen – saying that he had been arrested and taken away. The silly fellow refused to talk when the police asked what he was doing there, 'not to get you into trouble' he said! I suppose they thought it was suspicious, especially with his accent, so they went off with him. The worst of it all is that there is some idiotic research centre near there and they have lost a lot of guinea-pigs, and are accusing poor Tigran of having something to do with it. It is all quite mad but

Later

I was interrupted, and what with one thing and another I cannot remember how I was going to finish that sentence. Mrs Lockett has taken my letter to Harvey to the post, so would you please when you get this ring him up and ask him to come home, just for a few days? I really do need him, and I am sure he could get compassionate leave for a thing like this. Tell him that things have taken a turn for the worse, and that you really think he should come and help – I'm sure *you* could persuade him!

I have just spent a gruelling hour with a detective. The room is still full of smoke and after-shave. I should not have thought policemen were allowed to be so fragrant, unless they are acting as agents provocateurs. This one was really rather a nice young man with a touching desire to cut a good figure, but of course one does not know what is going on in their minds. I suppose he came because I had rung up the Home Secretary, several times, although I might have known *he* would be no help whatsoever. The detective wanted to know all about Tigran, how long I had known him, where we had met etc. I said he was an old friend of yours and you were an old friend of mine; then he suddenly asked about Uncle Hugo – *he* is supposed to be in Zambia, but as his flight has been delayed he is in fact still here, staying with Aunt Lucy, much against her will. He asked me where Uncle Hugo was and I quite truthfully said I did not know; he went out this morning heading for Gamages, but trackless wildernesses are more in Uncle Hugo's line than London Transport and really he could have been anywhere. The detective then asked whether Sir Hugo had given permission for 'this man Leontyev' to live in the cottage. I thought perhaps a small admission would make him feel more kindly towards me so I told him that it had been my idea, and that Uncle Hugo knew nothing about it. He seemed pleased, and so was I, as one is when one has given sugar to a horse. He then asked whether I knew that Tigran had not been alone at the cottage. I was terribly foxed by this so to change the subject I explained to him that Aunt Lucy (who thank God was asleep in her room) was a frail old lady and I did not want her to hear about this matter, and I tenderly begged him not to question her, and if he met her on his way out, not to tell her who he was. He said he would do what he could. Then suddenly he said rather crossly, 'You knew Tigran Leontyev well? One might say intimately?' Well, one knows what policemen mean by that, so I had to distract his attention again and I rather dramatically said that I would tell him everything I knew if *he* would tell *me* something: Where is Tigran? He told me straight away that he is in gaol in Manchester, that he was cheerful (this man had actually seen him!) but that he would not say anything, apart from the fact that he did not even know Crufty Research Centre existed. I felt excited when I knew he had actually seen Tigran, but then he suddenly said that things looked bad for him, that whoever broke into the Research Centre had an accomplice, a woman (how on earth could they know?), that women's clothes had been found in Uncle Hugo's cottage, and also certain implements that could have been used in the crime; he seemed terribly excited about a butterfly net.

All this time you must realise Aunt Lucy might have asked for me, Uncle Hugo might have come into the house, Mrs Lockett might have interrupted us with something utterly untoward; I thought I would finish off the whole stupid business so I told him that I was with Tigran the night the Research Centre was broken into, the clothes were mine, and that thus everything was explained. He seemed pleased, as well he might, at getting all this information and I thought he would go away and release Tigran and look elsewhere for the guinea-pig thief, but instead he went on asking silly questions such as did Tigran and I ever talk about politics; before he went I did extract a promise that he would keep to himself the fact that I had been at the cottage with Tigran, but I don't know how much such a promise is worth. I suppose poor Harvey will have to know the whole thing in the end.

As I was showing this wretched young man out, we met Uncle Hugo at the top of the stairs, giving his impersonation of a poor old man who can hardly put one foot before the other. He was panting and nodding his head in the most

convincing manner, and certainly did not look like a candidate for a plant-exploring expedition. The detective stepped aside respectfully, murmured 'After you, sir', and then ran lightly and energetically down the stairs, to demonstrate his comparative youth and agility. Thank goodness Uncle Hugo did not say anything (except that Gamages was staffed by muttonheads) which would have given him away. I could not have stood it if that young man had started all over again on Uncle Hugo, especially as I had encouraged the belief that he was already in Zambia.

I felt quite elated immediately after this, but now I am rather depressed, I feel I have not done anything except try to persuade Harvey to come and help. There are only a few days before the end of Tigran's holiday. I wonder whether you could do something over there about his firm? It is called United States Engineering Inc. If you could tell them *something* – that he had been taken ill – just so that they don't blame him if he does not get back on time.

I will write and let you know of any developments. Please impress on Harvey the urgency of all this – don't let him *think it over*, there isn't time. I am going out now to post this and to have a double at the pub on the corner, to help me face the rigours of the dinner-table.

Yours, Cornelia

Tigran Leontyev to Mrs Lamb July 4th

Darling Cornelia,

I hope you got my little letter, but anyway when you get this one you will know where I am. This prison is not bad but I hope to get out soon. They ask me every day about Research Centre but I know nothing. They ask me also about who was in cottage with me but I do not reply.

Nobody beat me and the food is quite good so I am okay but getting very bored. I hope they soon catch man who stole animals, then they will let me go. I thought of writing to U.S.E. (where I work) but thought perhaps this is not a very good address. It does not matter, I soon get another job when I get back to States.

Cheerioh darling, look after yourself,

Love and kisses, Tigran

What is guineapig? I never saw one.

Mrs Lamb to Tigran Leontyev Bede Street.
July 7th

Darling,

It was wonderful to get your letter but I do feel so dreadful about the whole thing and I do apologise to you from the bottom of my heart – it is all my fault for taking you to the cottage and for leaving you there. I have already told the police that I was there with you so there is no need to refuse to answer when they ask you. I am doing everything I possibly can to get you out, but the police are so obstinate, once they get an idea in their heads it is almost impossible to change it.

I have asked my husband to come back from New York and help us. I hope you do not mind, but he is very good at getting people out of trouble and he knows a lot of high-up people who would be able to help. I have tried the Home Secretary (do you remember we met him in the Belle Meunière?) without success. I am afraid he is the kind of man who thinks that the very fact that a woman asks for something means that it would probably be best to refuse. But I have asked Harvey to ring him up and I'm sure *he* will do better.

I don't know whether you see the newspapers in prison. I

believe they cut out all the interesting bits, so perhaps you have not seen the stories about the Crufty Research Centre, which you are supposed to have broken into. Apparently a lot of the guinea-pigs were not so much stolen as *sprung* and there are now guinea-pigs all over the county. (They are rather difficult to describe if you have never seen one, like a cross between a mouse and a rabbit, different colours and of limited intelligence.) The Ministry of Defence refuses to say what was being done to them at the Centre but one is glad they are free. They reproduce at an astonishing rate, so if it is true that 750 have been lost, they are going to become quite a feature of the Cheshire countryside. We are told in a furious article by an animal lover in this morning's paper, too, that some of them were pregnant. I hope they don't get as far as Uncle Hugo's garden and eat the roses. *You* are also mentioned in the newspaper but in rather a discreet way, and so far I don't think your name has come into it. I expect you are sub judice or something like that.

I have so far managed to protect Aunt Lucy from the whole business. *I* read the papers to her, and in any case it is not the sort of story she would be interested in. Scientific research does not touch her, and she considers the Ministry of Defence to be lax in having discontinued conscription, so she boycotts them as a subject for reading. She might be roused by the plight of the guinea-pigs, but her sight is not good enough for anything other than headlines, and they have not reached that eminence yet.

I suppose somebody will read this letter so I can't say all I would like to. I wonder if they let you smoke – I would love to send you some cigarettes and other things, but I don't know whether you would get them and in any case in a day or two I am sure you will be out – just as soon as Harvey begins operations. To the person who does read this, may I ask them to write and let me know whether I can write again? It would be very kind, as I do not know the rules about people in prison.

To you, darling Tigran, I will just say again how terribly sorry I am to have got you into all this trouble. I send you all my love.

Yours, Cornelia

Mrs Lamb to Harvey Lamb Bede Street.
July 8th

Darling Harvey,

It was lovely to talk to you last night, even though you were so stern and would not tell me how you are or what you are doing. I am very disappointed that you are not coming over – it would have been so nice to see you! But I do see how inconvenient it would be for you. I wish I could have persuaded you to telephone Peter rather than write. It really is urgent as I explained to you; and I don't see that it matters if Peter thinks we are flapping, as you call it. There are only two days to go but I am sure Peter could get Tigran out of prison and on to a plane in no time at all if he wanted to. Quite apart from Tigran losing his job, every day he is in gaol is on my conscience; I thought you were rather unkind about this last night. I do feel that it is my fault and after all Tigran has not done anything wrong. It is only red tape that is keeping him in; and I did so hope that you could cut it quickly. When you do write to Peter would you tell him to telephone me? He did promise to, last time I spoke to him, but he sounded so disapproving that I don't think I can rely on it.

Things are fairly gloomy here, hardly lightened at all by the fact that Uncle Hugo is supposed to be getting off at last tomorrow. This flat is not large enough for us all. It is like being cooped up with the two fighting wasps – however uninvolved, one is bound to get stung. It is a strain, too, keeping to myself all this worry about Tigran and wondering all the time whether some telephone call or intercepted letter may suddenly give the whole thing away. I suppose I should count myself lucky that Uncle Hugo never reads newspapers – he is rather grumpy, and I don't think he would take kindly to the idea of his cottage being the centre of so much interest. Aunt L. is in a reproachful mood; she has not forgiven me for staying away so long, and in fact is about to import a rival reader to put my nose out of joint. I don't think I *will* tell her all about it, in spite of your advice. It would be awfully complicated to explain and she might just possibly be very angry and throw me out, and I do want to stay here for the time being, in order to be on the spot for any developments, however uncomfortable it may be. Apart from other troubles, woodworm has been discovered in the welsh dresser and one of the dining-room chairs, and Aunt Lucy expects all the furniture in the flat to come crashing about our ears, eaten away from within. We are having a ceremonial visit from the Rentokil men tomorrow, for which all decks have to be cleared.

I may sound fairly cheerful, Harvey, but I am not. I tried to say this on the phone only you wouldn't let me: I really am *frightfully* sorry, about this whole thing. I didn't mean to get involved in anything like this – I mean in *anything*, not just all this trouble. But if you had not gone away and left me here it would not have happened, would it? I *do* wish you were here – and not just because you could help, either. You mustn't accuse me of not meaning things like that. You really were rather horrid on the telephone, but I suppose I deserve it.

Yours, Cornelia

Harvey Lamb to the Rt. Hon. Peter Bath, M.P. July 8th

Dear Peter,

I am sorry to bother you about this, but I understand my wife has been in touch with you about the case of Tigran Leontyev. I do not want to press you in any way, but I would be very grateful if you could let me know as much as is compatible with security about the progress of the case and its probable conclusion. I would also, of course, be eternally grateful if this business could be conducted with the maximum discretion. You can see how embarrassing it is for me.

Yours, Harvey

Peter Bath to Harvey Lamb Home Office.
July 14th

Dear Harvey,

Tigran Leontyev

I assume you already know the basic facts of this case. The position at the moment is that Leontyev is being held pending further investigations. He has been cleared by us, but the security people are working on something which apparently may take some time. Naturally we will do our best to keep the whole thing as discreet as possible. The publicity we have already had is extremely unwelcome to us and to Defence, and we are doing our best to deal with it.

I will keep in touch.

Yours, Peter

Mrs Lamb to Albert Minoprio Esq., M.P. July 15th

Dear Mr Minoprio,

I don't know whether you remember me, but we met at dinner at Margot Bassett's, about a year ago. We had a conversation about nature and artifice; everybody else was talking about George Brown. My husband is Harvey Lamb, who is in the foreign service in New York.

I am writing to you about Tigran Leontyev, an Armenian, who is in prison in Manchester. He is being held there on suspicion of having something to do with the theft of guinea-pigs from Crufty Research Centre, of which I know for a fact (and have told the police) that he is entirely innocent, but nevertheless they will not let him go. He has already lost his job in America as a result of being kept here, and so far as I can make out he is in prison *without trial.* I am sure you will feel that something should be done about this injustice. Tigran Leontyev is a hero of the Polish Resistance, an American citizen and completely harmless. I am writing to you about this because I know how hard you have fought to get wrongs righted and protect people who have no one else to stand up for them. Please do what you can.

Yours, Cornelia Lamb

Mrs Lamb to Mrs Nieman Bede Street.
July 15th

Darling Christiane,

I have had a letter from Tigran! He wrote to me from prison and I have written back, but it is difficult to write a letter which is going to be read by a lot of extraneous people – for instance I wanted to advise him not to try to escape, but I thought it might be misunderstood. He says he is well, and well-fed, but bored, which sounds a rather dangerous combination, considering the experience he has had in breaking out of jails. I would like to go up and see him, but at the moment I do not want to leave here in case any of the irons I have in the fire come to fruition, if you know what I mean.

I suppose you know that Harvey telephoned me, but it was a most unsatisfactory conversation. He won't come over; well, I don't blame him for that, but he was so calm about poor Tigran's predicament and wasted an enormous amount of telephone time asking about my part in the business. (Perhaps to be fair, it was I who wasted the time in trying to avoid a reply – unsuccessfully, as I suppose I should have expected.) I could *not* persuade him how important it is to act quickly – I should have thought that a sense of urgency was necessary in our dynamic society, but it seems singularly lacking in the Government service. I suppose the fact that policemen are not *allowed* to hurry proves that it is policy, not just preference on the part of the individuals. Now a week has passed since I spoke to Harvey and absolutely nothing is moving. I have rung up the Home Secretary several times and his answer is always the same, even in the same words, which gives one a macabre feeling of complete stasis. I am now trying to break this up by getting in touch with everybody I know who is even remotely influential, notably an ancient but fiery M.P. who has been famous from time immemorial for harrying Ministers, stirring up the readers of the *Daily Mirror* and turning out books with titles like *My Ninety Years of Struggle*. Everybody in public life respects him; they wish he would meet a sudden and honourable death. I met him at a dinner-party. He is a susceptible old bird, and I am sure I can persuade him to help.

Did you manage to do anything about United States Engineering? I am sure if you went to see them you could persuade them that Tigran will be back soon, and that they should keep his job open for him. Some of these companies are very paternal, and according to Tigran he was a great success there, so surely they will not want to lose him? When you next see Harvey, give him my love, and try to find out what he is doing; he might well tell you more than he will tell me.

Love, Cornelia

Mrs Bender to Harvey Lamb

Bede Street.
July 16th

My dear Harvey,

My promised monthly letter comes a little late, I am afraid – we are in a hugger-mugger here because Hugo is with me as well as Cornelia, which puts a great strain on our little household. Mrs Lockett is grappling with it as best she can, but sometimes I fear for her health. Hugo is on his way to Zambia but there has been some sort of muddle about his tickets and he does not seem to know when he will be off. I remember in the days when Neville and I used to travel, how simple and pleasant it all was. There was never the slightest difficulty in getting wherever one wanted to go, I suppose because in those days one only travelled if one really wanted to, whereas now everywhere is crowded with these dreadful people who simply want to be able to say they have been to a foreign country, though they would do so much better to stay at home. All these delays do not improve Hugo's temper. At the best of times he could never be patient. I tell him it would be far better to give up the trip altogether, but of course he will not listen.

Cornelia is well and happy. She has just spent nearly a fortnight with Mary Nash and her family. It must have been terribly hard work as Mary was ill in bed and Larry had broken his leg and could not do much to help. I am not happy about her going there – they seem to live such a rough-and-tumble life. Once again she had several bruises, on her arms, neck and shoulders. She told me the children had been playing about in their father's studio and one of them had accidentally hit her with a hammer. I tell her she looks as though she had been playing with bear cubs rather than children. But of course Mary's have always been *quite* ungovernable, stuffed with orange juice and vitamins, and allowed to do just as they like. And nowdays one cannot even count on their behaving any better as they grow older. I have made Cornelia promise that she will not go down again – it is really asking too much of her good nature to expect her to drop everything and go all that way simply because Mary is indisposed. There is such a thing as being too accommodating – people take advantage of it. I think Cornelia takes my point. At any rate she has assured me she has no intention of going down there again for some time. She seems rather quiet – I think she is missing you. I have twice heard her asking Mrs Lockett whether the post had come, so you see she is thinking of you, and perhaps hoping you will break your resolution and write to her. But I know that once you have made a plan you stick to it – you are like your dear father in that. It is unfortunate that you should have been posted to New York just at this time. The so-called American way of life is *not* conducive to happy marriage even for people as stable as yourself. I suppose there is not the slightest hope of your being transferred to somewhere more civilised?

Have you come across Gervase Stone while you have been in New York? Do look him up if you can, he was such a dear friend of your father's, although he has been out there so long that perhaps now he has become completely Americanised. I believe he went into oil. He was always very keen, and sank a well near his house in Leicestershire, which caused his neighbour's garden to subside. In America, where I understand they do not have gardens, he will of course be better off.

I hope all goes well with you, my dear boy. I will write again, as I promised.

Your affectionate aunt, Lucy.

Albert Minoprio, M.P., to Mrs Lamb

House of Commons.
July 18th

Dear Mrs Lamb,

Thank you for calling my attention to the case of Tigran Leontyev. If an injustice has been done it shall be righted.

Yours sincerely, Albert Minoprio

From the 'Daily Mirror', July 27th

Tigran Leontyev is a name you will not have heard of. A name difficult to pronounce.

But it is a name we are not ashamed to put before you, and to repeat, in the cause of justice.

For Tigran Leontyev is in jail. He has been there for six weeks. And the charge? There is no charge. There is only the suspicion that he broke into the Defence Research Centre at Crufty, near which he was found.

This man is not British. Admittedly.

But he is Polish. And a citizen of the United States of America.

During the war he fought the common enemy. A proud member of the Resistance Movement, he risked his life a thousand times a day in his years-long battle with the dreaded Gestapo.

He was imprisoned, tortured, and beaten, for the cause in which he, and we, passionately believed.

Now he is in prison again, and in this freedom-loving country of ours.

Proofs of his innocence abound.

But he has no one to defend him. Only this newspaper, and you, its readers, who hate injustice and will protect its victims, no matter who they are.

So we warn the powers that be. Free this man, or you will have us to reckon with!

Mrs Lamb to Mrs Nieman Bede Street.
July 30th

My dear Christiane,

I thought you would like to see these press cuttings about Tigran. And it would do no harm if Harvey saw them. He won't like it, but after all if he had done as I asked and telephoned Peter Bath at once, everything could have been cleared up in what he would consider a gentlemanly way. Harvey has always been completely reliable, but I must say I am beginning to wonder whether he ever wrote to Peter at all. *He* keeps saying 'It is rather a complex matter' or 'I wish you would leave it with me', and when I asked him straight out whether he had heard from Harvey he seemed to think it was an indiscreet question. I tried coaxing him and I tried being pathetic but he is a perfect stone. Now that Home Secretaries no longer have lists of condemned people on their mantelpieces and have to steel themselves against reprieves, I don't see the necessity to choose anybody *quite* so immovable for the job. In the end I threatened him. I said what if it got into the papers that a hero of the Resistance Movement was languishing in jail on a trumped-up charge? He suddenly came off his official manner and said, 'Now, Cornelia, I hope you will not talk about this business – think of Harvey!' I said I would not talk about it, if he would do something about it. Then he said again it was a complex matter and that I didn't realise what was involved. I said it involved a large, active man being shut up in a little cell, but he gets terribly embarrassed when I talk about Tigran, I could practically hear him blushing. People like that make me furious. In the end he got quite shirty and said I was doing more harm than good by my persistence. He was really quite unpleasant. It is true that the monthly trade figures are due out soon and an economist I met said they were perfectly frightful, so I suppose all ministers are suffering from pre-menstrual tension, but just the same I don't think it excuses him. Just after this telephone conversation I happened to go round to Margot Bassett's for a drink and although I didn't really intend to, I told Murray Bassett all about it. He said he might get his paper to send somebody along, to see whether there was a story in it. These are the results. As you see, poor Tigran has been remanded in custody again. I wish I could go up and see him but at the moment I can't get away from here, partly because I am rather short of money. Harvey pays me an allowance, but I bought rather a sumptuous collection of clothes this summer and I am only just managing to keep my overdraft below bank managers' eye-level. I suppose I can't keep Aunt Lucy in the dark for ever; Harvey wants me to make a *clean breast* of it (as though I were made of marble and could be scrubbed) but I don't feel inclined to do so. She might throw me out. She is unpredictable at the best of times where questions of behaviour are concerned, and this could not be described as the best of times. Uncle Hugo has gone off at last to Zambia, but has left behind him proofs of iniquity which will preclude him (she says) from ever setting foot here again. We have recently had the Rentokil men in to save the furniture from imminent collapse through woodworm; only to discover at the end of an expensive hour that Uncle Hugo was, as it were, the invisible worm. He had certainly fled in the night: and left behind him little pools of sawdust at strategic places in the furniture and under it. We found the proof – a little bag of the stuff at the back of a shelf in his wardrobe. For some reason I come in for some of the obloquy, probably because I have never really been forgiven for my frequent visits to Mary Nash, in spite of their being errands of mercy. Mrs Lockett doesn't come off much better. It was she who raised the alarm, and discovered the vital clue in the wardrobe; and she is being treated as the emissary who is hanged for bringing bad news. In fact, only Klara Meiss is persona grata. She is an agamous lady of German extraction who was brought in, when I was least in favour, to take on the duties I was neglecting. She comes almost every day. She reads aloud and runs errands and listens with a positively embarrassing degree of attention to stories about the past. It is like those innocents from another world coming into 'so-called civilisation' and hearing 'It's a Long Way to Tipperary' for the first time. Occasionally she has lunch or tea with us and lavishes indiscriminate praise, no matter what Mrs Lockett's culinary mood. Today we had a dish which I call karate chops, and she wrestled with knife and fork between politeness and greed, down to the last fibre. I am sometimes forced to be present when she is reading aloud – perhaps to improve my own performance. She can certainly give me points on fidelity to the text; she reads misprints like an Indian tailor copying holes. Yesterday, reading from *The Times* she announced that 'Mr Heath wants to have another erection this year'. Aunt Lucy murmured, 'Dear me, I hope not,' whereupon she read on, with no further comment from either side. Even to typescript she has the same blind obedience. Spencer has written a play in verse which he sent to Aunt Lucy, and as he has a tendency to cry when reading his own work, the task fell on

Klara. I was to stand by, and perhaps take a role. But as there was seldom more than one person on stage at a time, I became instead a member of the audience. It was painful, as I expect Aunt Lucy intended it to be. Klara minces her words; they go through the grinder of a residual Teutonic accent. It was horrible to see the thick wad of typescript, the pages turning so slowly as Klara enunciated every syllable, even prefacing the stage directions with 'Brecket'. Her textual fidelity was put to the test: 'Brecket. He gets up and pees through the window.' Spencer's R must be stiff. Before the end of the play the hero had 'entered the room and peed all round him' and also 'peed down the dark stairs'. Aunt Lucy makes no comment, but whether she is sparing Klara's feelings or simply not listening I don't know.

I was hoping that Klara Meiss would satisfy Aunt Lucy's craving for human companionship and would attend to the emergencies which always seem to arise when I have arranged to go out, such as the absolute necessity to get the famille rose out of the top cupboard and make sure it is all there. But I find I am still necessary, on these occasions. 'It's all hands to the pump,' Aunt Lucy cries cheerfully; with a correspondingly dramatic change of mood when she discovers I am not to be one of the pumpers. I have to face her reproaches quite often, as I have come out of retirement now that I have been to Margot's house, and I am going out to dinner quite a lot. Returning this hospitality presents a problem. I can't afford restaurants, and not everybody would appreciate an evening with Aunt Lucy and Major Markette.

Mrs Lockett has just put her head into my room to summon me to the drawing-room; tomorrow Aunt Lucy is going shopping and the strategy has to be arranged. I hope we chance upon a magnanimous taxi-man. Last time, she asked one to drive slowly along Bond Street so that she could look at the shops, and twice urged him to 'be bold' and go the wrong way up one-way streets, in order to save paying for the longer way round.

I send my kind regards to Harvey. I don't think he deserves love.

Yours, Cornelia

The Rt. Hon. Peter Bath to Harvey Lamb Home Office.
August 10th

Dear Harvey,

I am writing to you with regard to the case of Tigran Leontyev. I am sorry to say that since I wrote to you in July, the position has deteriorated. There has been a good deal of publicity in the press and on television and radio, both as regards Leontyev's continued stay in custody, and the activities of the Crufty Research Centre, with the result that we are being pressed from two sides on this matter. Minoprio has somehow got hold of it and you know what that means. He is asking a question in the House on Tuesday, and Mortimer Westlake, who, as you know, represents animals' interests, is also raising the matter. The Animals' Defence Association is organising a march to Downing Street on Sunday with a petition, and we have had representations from the American Embassy and also from the Armenian and Polish communities in this country. I have myself been approached several times by the Council for Civil Liberties. I had a word with the Defence Secretary again last night and he tells me that one of his Permanent Secretaries, Charles Dawtry, has a personal interest in the case and would like more urgent action taken. We have of course to await Security's report on the matter, but in the meantime we wish to minimise public anxiety, and I am bound to say that I feel that your wife could help here. I have had several conversations with her on the subject, all of which have been somewhat unsatisfactory, and something she said on the last occasion suggested that she may have been the cause of the matter getting into the press in the first place. I believe Murray Bassett is a personal friend of your family, and I fear she may have been indiscreet. I have done my best to impress upon her the necessity for discretion in such a delicate matter, but I do not feel that she fully understands the gravity of the situation, and I am therefore writing to ask whether you would get in touch with her as soon as possible before any more damage is done. I am sorry to have to write to you on such an embarrassing matter. This letter is, of course, strictly personal and completely off the record.

Yours, Peter

Mrs Nieman to Mrs Lamb *New York.*
August 15th

Dear Cornelia,

I am not surprised to hear of these disasters, I told you no good would come from keeping Leontyev in England when he ought to be going to Paris. I had no intention to show the cuttings to Harvey, but he already saw them. He reads the English papers and also he has a letter from Mr Bath which tells him everything. He came to see me today and all he says is, 'Well, Christiane, your friend Cornelia has really excelled herself,' and although he is calm and even smiles, I know he is very angry and I think he suffers too. He looks sad. And to call you *my friend*, does that not suggest that you have lost him? I do not wonder at it, Englishmen do not like to be embarrassed.

I have also had to deal with Angélique. She told me her

parents liked Tigran but wondered that he left Paris so quickly. Angélique naturally expected him back here long ago and at last I had to tell her that he was in trouble with the police and could not leave England. That is the end for her, she is through with him and I cannot blame her. She wants to see him when he gets back, to tell him personally she is through – she will like to have one more emotional scene. I think he gets a rough time, she is a strong girl and sometimes very bad-tempered.

I have my troubles. Melville has a new friend, a very young man in spectacles from another law office. He comes here often and is excessively polite to me, as though I was older than both of them. Melville also treats him politely; last night he got up when he came into the room. I suppose when he starts holding the door for him I should begin to worry. Luckily, our vacation comes soon. We will go to Maine and see Mel's parents, who never have noticed anything strange about him. We will have terrible food, which always makes Mel fonder of me.

Yours, Christiane

Harvey Lamb to Mrs Lamb

New York.
August 16th

Dear Cornelia,

I have had a most disturbing letter from Peter Bath about the case of your Armenian friend. You may remember that when we talked on the telephone in July, I asked you to leave it to myself and to Peter to take any necessary action, and I cannot understand why you have completely ignored this advice. Peter tells me that Albert Minoprio and Mortimer Westlake have both raised questions in the House, and I gather from what he said that you have also approached Charles Dawtry and Murray Bassett. You mentioned in your letter of the 3rd July various people who might be asked for help, but you said you would not do so without my permission. I cannot imagine what has induced you to go back on this, when you must realise how painful the whole thing is for me from the personal point of view and inexpressibly more so now that it has become a public concern. It would not have done so if it had not been for you, and this makes my position vis-à-vis Peter Bath extremely embarrassing. Besides this, as you must surely realise, Security is involved, and if your name should be brought into it, my career may well be ruined.

It is too late to repair the damage that has already been done, but I must insist that you stop this lobbying at once, and say nothing more to anyone else about the matter. I have given Peter Bath an absolute assurance that you will take no more part in this business, and I expect you to honour it.

Yours, Harvey

Mrs Lamb to Harvey Lamb

Bede Street.
August 15th

Dear Harvey,

It's all very well to talk about your position but what about Tigran's? He has been in prison for weeks on the trumped-up charge that he broke into Uncle Hugo's cottage, which he only did anyway because I told him to. He has lost his job and might never get another one after this, and he is probably being ill-treated as well. It is not my fault if there is a public scandal about it – I should never have said anything if it had not been for Peter Bath's *total immobility*, and you may tell him that when you write to him – it is no use my telling him as he never listens to anything I say. You are very unfair about my lobbying, as you call it. I did write to Albert Minoprio, but I have never even seen Mortimer Westlake. I told Murray about it at a party, but after all it was not his paper who made such an issue of it. I haven't said anything yet to Robert Moxon and I only just asked Charles Dawtry to mention it to his Minister – surely that was not indiscreet? I would not have done any of these things if you had come over, as I asked you to, and pulled strings. As you did not, *I* had to pull them, and if it gets Tigran out of prison quickly, I am not sorry. I'm sure you need not worry about your career. After all, you have not been involved, and are not likely to be. And please do not give Peter Bath assurances on my behalf. If it was the other way round and *I* promised somebody that *you* would do something, wouldn't you think it absurd?

Yours, Cornelia

Mrs Bender to Harvey Lamb Bede Street.
August 27th

My dear Harvey,

I am afraid I have bad news of Cornelia. She has insisted on rushing off to Wood Cottage, quite alone, and will not say how long she expects to be away. More extraordinary still, she has hired a car to drive herself up there, the height of extravagance when there is a perfectly good train and bus service. Of course I tried to dissuade her but she would not listen. I do not know what she means by wanting a little rest, her life with me here is leisurely in the extreme, and I thought she was happy and comfortable. Her behaviour *has* been a little odd lately, she has seemed unsettled and even – I can say it to *you*! – a little difficult. She has been keeping to her room more than usual, and tried to hide from me the fact that she had received a letter from you. I should never have known, if I had not recognised your hand on the envelope. She knows how interested I am in all your doings, yet she would tell me nothing of what was in it. I have had a long talk with Dr Dench about her and I shall get him to look at her when she comes back. It is the greatest of pities that there is no telephone at Wood Cottage – as you know I never tired of telling Hugo that he should have one installed. I knew something like this would happen some day to justify me. However, she has promised to write to me and I will let you know as soon as she does so. In the meantime, please do not worry too much. I am sure she will not stay long – she cannot know how uncomfortable the cottage is, and I think she will soon regret her impulsive flight.

I too have my troubles but I will not worry you with these. One piece of bad news in a letter is enough. I hope all goes well at least with you, my dear boy.

Your affectionate aunt, Lucy

Mrs Lamb to Mrs Nieman

Wood Cottage,
Pigpound Lane.
August 28th

My dear Christiane,

As you see I have fled to the bosom of the country, partly to escape from Aunt Lucy and partly because I am going to try to see Tigran. Life at Bede Street has not been at its best lately and took a dramatic turn for the worse last Thursday when Aunt Lucy received a message from Spencer, the favourite poet: he had been married, by some parson or parsons unknown, the previous Saturday! It was a bombshell – one of the anti-personnel sort, whose splinters lacerate innocent bystanders for miles around. None of us escaped, with the possible exception of Klara Meiss, and she, I imagine, has had to call on every grain of Teutonic discipline to withstand the assault. Meals were hell. If I was alone with Aunt Lucy I was exposed to the full flood of her disappointment and the malevolence that goes with it, which though primarily aimed at Spencer's girl-friend, has secondary targets among Aunt Lucy's acquaintance – fiends in human shape who have ruined the careers of countless good men simply by marrying them. If Klara were there – and during the period of mourning there have been reckless invitations to lunch – emotion was somewhat contained in deference to the presence of an outsider, but then on the other hand I have to watch Klara eat. Sometimes she mashes everything up for all the world as though she had been at Rugby; she always eats everything, whittling bones and scouring plates as though determined to demonstrate her intense appreciation. The day before I left we had trout and in no time the backbone looked as though white ants had been through it, and then she put its head into her mouth; it disappeared, looking resigned, with its closed sleepy eyes, and reappeared sucked dry, one supposes of all nutrition. I have fled from such scenes, engendering, of course, a pall or miasma of reproach in which I simply had to grope my way about, hoping to stumble upon something that would please. I can't describe to you the power of Aunt Lucy's moral pressure when she disapproves of something – I almost abandoned the plan from sheer weakness. The evening before I left was truly terrible; 'your last evening', Aunt Lucy called it, as though my execution had been fixed for dawn. To celebrate the occasion Klara, invading the kitchen during Mrs Lockett's day off, had made what I can only call a Sacher-Masoch Torte, which we were forced to eat by Aunt Lucy's pitiless power. I suppose while I'm away, Klara will step into my shoes. When she came into my room once, sent with a message by Aunt Lucy, she clasped her hands and cried, 'Oh what a dear little room!' surveying with affection the furniture from the servants' rooms in Gloucestershire, which I am sure she would be glad to inherit. When I go back I may well find myself cast out, like Uncle Hugo, though I don't think I have reached his level in the unpopularity poll yet. But perhaps my ingratitude and thoughtlessness make me eligible for the gallery of women who have been ruinous to good men. Aunt Lucy referred to 'poor Harvey' several times during the evening. If I quarrel with Aunt Lucy I shall have to ask Harvey for money, and as I have just written him rather an angry letter, I certainly don't want to do that. All the same, I simply had to come up here, and now, in the silence of Uncle Hugo's roseleaf-darkened sitting-room, I feel calm and passive, waiting to be disapproved of by Harvey still more, when he learns where I am. Tomorrow I am going to try to see Tigran. I shall give him your love, and Angélique's too if he seems to need it. She must be an unworthy girl, to throw him over for such a trivial reason; it ought to make her love him all the more, and you may tell her so. Do write to me – here, if you like. The postman is a charming man and is more likely to forward letters to me chez Aunt Lucy than the other way about.

Yours, Cornelia

Harvey Lamb to Mrs Lamb New York.
August 29th

Dear Cornelia,

I am very sorry to see the attitude your letter of August 15th reflects. What you do not seem to realise is that you are doing your friend Leontyev no good. If you had not raised a public hullabaloo he might well have been quietly released by now. But once pressure is put upon the authorities and publicity focused upon them, they often have to act more strictly than they might have done otherwise.

I notice that you say that you have not yet mentioned the matter to Robert Moxon. May I beg you very very earnestly not to approach him, or anyone else. No good would come of it. Everything is being done to settle this case quickly and any further move from you would only delay matters. So may I ask you to take no further action, for my sake? It is causing me a great deal of distress and worry and it would be a great relief to me if you would write and let me have an assurance that you have understood the situation as I have described it, and will do nothing to aggravate it.

Yours, Harvey

Mrs Lamb to Mrs Nieman Wood Cottage.
September 5th

Darling Christiane,

It is not very long since I wrote to you, but guess who is sitting beside me? Tigran Leontyev, larger, much larger, than life! It is a long story, but I must tell you the whole of it, because it reflects so much credit on myself. You may tell parts of it to Harvey, but only parts – I will tell you which, when I have finished.

The very first day I was here I went for a walk, and in a field I found a little girl with long hair, busily engaged in pulling up snares, quietly cursing somebody as she did so. When she saw me she looked very fierce and asked me who I was, as though I was trespassing, but when I offered to help her grub up the snares she became more amiable and let me walk with her while she told me what a terrible time she had coming out here every day, going into the woodlands to frighten the squirrels away before the gunmen came, and getting up in the middle of the night to let off mousetraps. When we had walked for about half an hour she asked if I had any money, and then proposed we should go to a bakery where they make doughnuts. It was an enchanting place, in the side of a hill. They were just taking them out of the oven and she ate five. The baker gave us each a mug of tea and we sat down on a stone to recover while the child explained to me about the balance of nature.

On the way home we introduced ourselves. She turned out to be the daughter of Colonel Sapling, a friend of Uncle Hugo's, and we began to talk about the Great Guinea-pig Robbery. Up to now she had been rather a silent child but excess of doughnuts had loosened her tongue and she chattered gleefully about the police and newspaper reporters, every one of whom she seemed to have thwarted in some way and was glad of it. I naturally talked about Tigran and when she said 'I feel sorry for him', soberly, as though there *were* human beings who deserved sympathy, I suddenly had a flash of intuition. Without stopping to think I said, 'You let them out, didn't you?' She denied it furiously, but became very pink and sulky. I felt like Holmes in the last chapter, but I tried to be calm. I lured her into the cottage by talking about hedgehogs, and once there gave her some sherry. She was thirsty, and swigged down two glasses, and then she told me all about it. She is a sort of female, country Rififi. She made me swear the most gruesome oaths not to tell anybody (I don't think you count, on the other side of the Atlantic) because she had an accomplice, a boy, whose life would be *completely ruined* if his part in the business was ever found out. After an immense battle she at last agreed to let me ask the police whether some sort of bargain could be struck – I would tell them who did it, only if they would promise not to implicate the boy. The child argued that this was the sort of thing that happened on the telly and therefore could not be done in real life; but at last she gave in and I ran – literally – to the Police Station to start negotiations. It took hours, days, in fact, of frustrating and repetitive conversations with a succession of people, who all had to have it told from the beginning, like children listening to a favourite fairy story. We were hampered at first by the fact that the child stipulated that her father must not be told. She made great play with his widowerhood, and assured us she would be orphaned at once if he should learn of her peculiar activities and her familiarity with the inside of the Police Station. But it all ended happily. Tigran is released, the Civil Liberties people are congratulating themselves, and the *Daily Mirror* has an article headlined 'We've Won!' The only shade thrown on this dazzling dénouement is that Tigran has to get back to the States next week, and in the meantime we have completely run out of money. I have written to Margot asking her to lend me some, but there is no certainty that she will, and we are living, as they say, from hand to mouth, and are thinking of getting Pansy Sapling to rob a bank.

Tigran sends his love. He is going to the Post Office to post this and to telephone to his Uncle Woronowski, who wrote him a twelve-page letter while in jail, which irritated his captors, as they had no one to translate it. In the end Tigran translated it for them himself, reading it out in English to two policemen who, he said, were very much impressed by Uncle Woronowski's philosophy.

We have spent most of yesterday hiding from reporters, sitting in Colonel Sapling's attic like King Charles and Flora Macdonald. They were all over the place – when we came back to the cottage we sent Pansy Sapling on ahead, and she found one in the kitchen. She disposed of him by saying that Tigran had gone to catch a train, and giving him a true but uncomfortable route by footpath to the station. Today there has been a providential scandal about amorous milkmen on the new housing estate at Chorlton-cum-Hardy, and a lot of them have gone streaming off there, baying cheerfully. I managed to keep out of their way; luckily this cottage has several windows one cannot see through at all.

Tigran is a sort of hero in the village. People come up to him, stand very close and say loudly '*We* think,' pointing at themselves, 'that *you*'' pointing at him, 'are all right. Good man!' He has gratefully accepted this proferred refuge and just smiles and makes some suitable reply in Russian.

I suppose I ought really to be writing to Harvey and not to you, but I daresay he will hear the news from some unpolluted source such as Peter Bath. If not, you may tell him the case is solved, and even how I solved it, but please don't tell him I am staying at the cottage with Tigran. I don't want him to have anything else to reproach me with, and in four or five days' time, malheureusement, I shall be back in London, living a blameless life. Do write to me there.

Yours, Cornelia

Mrs Nieman to Mrs Lamb New York. September 9th

Dear Cornelia,

I have to tell you that Melville left me. He eloped with Earl Custance, the young man I told you about, who came here so often to eat my good dinners. I do not know where they are. Mel said in the note he left that they were going on a short vacation. He can surely not take him to his parents in Maine, though God knows he is crazy enough. Harvey is a great comfort to me, he advices me what to do and he is always right. He is cheerful, despite of his own troubles and his work at United Nations which at the moment is very hard.

Thank you for your letter, I am sorry for all your troubles though right now they don't seem as great as mine. I do not understand what you say about Angélique, I do not think he has done anything to make her love him, quite the reverse. She calls me quite often and always asks when he will go back so that she can revenge herself on him. Personally I do not think he deserves such interest. She already has a new friend, an Arabian prince who gives her a Cadillac and a cigarette lighter stuck all over with diamonds and rubies. These things she does not need, but they are reassuring, after her experience with Leontyev.

I will write you again when I am in more good spirits.

Yours, Christiane

Mrs Lamb to Mrs Nieman

Bede Street.
September 14th

Darling Christiane,

I am so sorry to hear from your letter – which crossed with mine – that Melville has left you. He will regret it, of course, in no time at all, so you had better make up your mind how you are going to receive him when he comes back.

As you see, I am back in Bede Street, though not entirely in Aunt Lucy's good graces. She considers my having spent a few days at Uncle Hugo's cottage as quite extraordinary; she asked Doctor Dench to tea to look me over discreetly for signs of insanity and she says 'You *look* quite well dear,' as though wondering at the deceptiveness of appearances. Klara Meiss is still in evidence, although I am glad to say I have not had to share the dinner-table with her since I came back. I am rather surprised that she has not stepped into my shoes while I was away – I am sure she would like to, although her friendly manner is quite impenetrable. She is all smiles, always addresses me as 'Mrs Lem' and I think disapproves of me deeply – the more since I made a slightly rash attempt to get her to agree to some sort of division of labour; after a gruelling reading (by her) in the Bonnie Prince Charlie sector, and then compulsory attendance for both of us at the Forsyte Saga, I suggested we might arrange to share the duties. 'Dewtees?' she said, opening her eyes very wide. 'For me it is all pleasure!' I am not quite willing to hand over to her altogether – I do not exactly know why. It is partly because I think Aunt Lucy wants me to stay, and in spite of everything there is a mysterious compulsion to please her, and partly (something to do with Tigran not being here any more) a desire to sit quietly in my burrow for a bit, rather than go out into the world. If I took a flat I should have to take a job, too, to bridge the gap between Harvey's bankers' orders – as it is, they are mortgaged for some months ahead because I borrowed some money from Margot Bassett and have also been straining the courtesy of various Accounts Departments for some time now. However, I am determined to lead a quiet and sedate life, and the clothes I have bought to console myself are not nearly as expensive as those I bought to celebrate. As long as Margot Bassett doesn't have to show Murray her bank statements, I shall be safe for some time.

Please don't tell Harvey any of this. He will either fuss about the amount of money he gives me, or else blame me for being extravagant, and I don't want him to do either. If I did move out of Bede Street, of course, I would let him know, though perhaps he is too cross with me to care?

I hope you are not too preoccupied with your own troubles to write to me. I should like to hear how Tigran gets on, what happened when he saw Angélique, and whether he got his job back. He went home practically penniless, a state which is all very well in Pott Shrigley but would not suit New York. He seemed quite cheerful about it and said his friends would help him – I hope it is true. I think I am more likely to get an accurate account from you than from him – in any case I have an idea he is not a very good correspondent.

I must end, as I am called to a conference with Aunt Lucy. Social life has begun again, after the crushing blow of Spencer's marriage, and tomorrow we are having a wake for the bride. Our numbers are to be made up by Roylance Cowlinshaw and Major Markette, so if you disapprove of me, Christiane, you can see that at least I am not going unpunished.

Yours, Cornelia

Mrs Bender to Harvey Lamb Bede Street.
September 15th

My dear Harvey,

I hasten to write and tell you that Cornelia is back! She does not seem any the worse for it, although a little *piano*. I daresay she feels rather ashamed at the discovery that I was perfectly right in thinking that she would not want to stay very long alone in that dreadful cottage – apparently it is as dark and uncomfortable as ever, though Cornelia insists that she enjoyed herself there – she does have a little trouble sometimes in admitting herself to be in the wrong!

I am very relieved to have her back – I have had troubles of my own which have made my anxiety about Cornelia all the harder to bear. Spencer has made a most unfortunate marriage. You know how interested I have been in his career and it is indeed sad to see it blighted so early. She is not at all a suitable girl, quite ignorant, and from the point of view of his career in the Ministry of Agriculture and Fisheries, it is far too young to marry. But, of course, one can say nothing. One can only stand by and watch the disaster, such is the powerlessness of friendship!

It would cheer me to have a letter from you, although I am sure your work takes up most of your time. I hope you are not overdoing it, and that you are finding life out there not too unpleasant. I have a most charming woman who is coming in now to read to me – taking over, I fear, some of Cornelia's duties! – and I try to get as much news from America as possible, so that I can visualise what you are up against. There have been some dreadful accounts recently about life in New York, and I regretted that I had not *insisted* on your taking my pistol. I would send it to you if you wish, but I believe you can buy a gun in any shop there, and I advise you to do so at once and to carry it with you. I understand it is a commonplace to be held up and robbed in broad daylight and that you cannot expect anyone to help you, or even take any notice. Here, we have not quite reached that stage but things are bad enough. You read of dreadful cases every day, and I am always glad to think I am armed. Beside my gun, I have kept several of the long hatpins we used to wear long ago, and which we always considered a good defence, if one was forced to go into some rough district. Major Markette says they can kill with ease, so long as you choose the right place to strike, just between the ribs.

I have heard nothing from Hugo, and in spite of everything I cannot help being anxious. I am afraid he is not fit *mentally* for such an expedition. But, of course, there is nothing to be done. He would go. And I suppose it will be weeks before I hear anything from him. He has always been the same – I remember how poor Mother suffered when he used to go to the Lake District and remain away for weeks at a time, completely out of touch with everyone. He is one of those unfortunate people – or perhaps one should call them fortunate! – who have no conception of other people's feelings.

I notice that you have written again to Cornelia lately – does this mean that your resolution not to write to her has broken down? Perhaps you are wise – it may be that anxiety about you and your marriage is partly the cause of her peculiar behaviour. I shall continue my monthly bulletins, however, and hope very much to get a reply from you soon.

Your affectionate aunt, Lucy

Mrs Lamb to Tigran Leontyev

Bede Street.
September 16th

Darling Tigran,

It seems a long time since I saw you. I do hope everything is all right in New York – that you still have your apartment and have got a splendid new job; and that you will come back soon! I miss you very much. I went to the National Portrait Gallery the day before yesterday and enclose a postcard of Mr Landseer's Lionhouse, where we used to meet.

Life with Aunt Lucy is much the same as ever it was and I am trying to take my part enthusiastically in its dramas. We had a dinner-party last night for the poet Spencer, his new wife, Major Markette and Roylance Cowlinshaw, who, by the way, sends his kind regards. Aunt Lucy took immense trouble over this funereal feast, excitedly cutting down the poundage of vegetables and the number of eggs needed for the sweet until Mrs Lockett was driven to me for my usual private advice: to use eight eggs and pretend to have used two. Mrs Lockett said, 'Oooh I don't like to deceive the old lady' but she did so, and had to suffer the penalty of keeping silent when Aunt Lucy triumphantly declared herself proved right – that two eggs would be *quite* enough. Linda arrived looking as though she were trying to hide behind her hair and every available ruffle and frill on her dress; she had successfully concealed herself to the knee with white boots which, as before, Aunt Lucy invited her to leave in the hall, supposing that it had come on to rain. The girl declined with so much energy that a bow flew out of her hair, which Aunt Lucy picked up, and offered to replace. The girl backed away – Aunt Lucy advanced. I have seen her in the same attitude and with the same expression with a bridle in her hand in a field in Gloucestershire. She grasped the forelock and pinned it firmly back, exposing an alarmed forehead but not, as perhaps she expected, the mark of Cain. Linda is one of those girls who pull their own hair and she missed her fringe all evening, but she did not undo Aunt Lucy's work. I cannot imagine where Spencer found a girl who is so easily intimidated. *He* behaved as though Linda did not belong to him and ran about for Aunt Lucy as usual. Major Markette was his familiar appalling self. He always has some particular target for his malice – this time it was students who sit in. They should be locked in, he says, and left there. The doors should be *welded*, he said, his eyes positively gleaming with hatred. Last time I saw him his enemies were, for some reason, young men who use the firm's car for taking their girl-friends out. For Major Markette there are no degrees of culpability: everyone who offends deserves the death penalty – in fact if he had his way nobody would escape it, except perhaps retired Army Officers and old gentlewomen. Roylance Cowlinshaw asked me where you had got to, and I told him you had gone back to America and that I wished you had not. 'Are you in love with him?' he asked like an amiable old rat hoping for a titbit. I felt inclined to tell him the whole story, if I had not thought he might regale Aunt Lucy with it some winter evening. We couldn't talk about you for long – Aunt Lucy likes general conversation, so I was saved from an indiscretion. Aunt Lucy was particularly regal, wearing her emeralds and sitting in the armchair, which puts her just out of reach of all the little things she might want, so as to give the maximum opportunity for gallantry. Spencer sat at her feet on the pouffe, Roylance earned his dinner by sitting beside Linda on the sofa. His attitude to Spencer's volte-face is one of scornful tolerance, rather like an amateur towards one who has turned pro. He is a nice old thing – do you remember him saying he wanted to paint your portrait? I wish he had – we might have taken it to the Portrait Gallery and hung it beside Tittle's Conrad.

Pansy Sapling is mounting a ferocious campaign against the local hunt and the farmers who shoot squirrels and is perfecting a trap for people who set traps – she sent me a diagram of it which rivals some of the more complicated structures of Leonardo da Vinci. She is learning the value of publicity and in spite of the short shrift she gave the reporters when she was protecting us from their attentions, now seems to have captured several of those young men who expose the seamy side of our national life. Her implication in our affair at Crufty got a good deal of publicity which enraged the Colonel, but it had a happy ending: you will be glad to know that her fine was paid – with some over – by the readers of the *News of the World*.

Dear Tigran, I love you. Write to me soon.

Your Cornelia

Harvey Lamb to Mrs Lamb New York. September 20th

Dear Cornelia,

I am sorry to hear that you are in financial difficulties. I am enclosing a cheque which should cover your immediate needs, and hope that now you are back with Aunt Lucy you will be able to live within your allowance.

I have heard from Peter Bath that the business about which we corresponded in August has been cleared up, at least so far as you are concerned. For me, of course, the consequences may still be serious, and I hope you now realise how foolish and unnecessary your intervention was, and how much damage can be done by acting without full knowledge of the facts.

Christiane sends her love.

Yours, Harvey

Mrs Lamb to Mrs Nieman Bede Street. September 25th

Dear Christiane,

I am absolutely furious with you – I *told* you not to tell Harvey that I was short of money. Now he has sent me an enormous cheque which is quite unnecessary as I could easily have paid Margot Bassett and the other people given time. It is obvious too that Harvey knows that I had been with Tigran at Wood Cottage again – I think I asked you particularly not to tell him this and I am very surprised at your being so unreliable. I do think there are times when you ought to restrain yourself from running other people's lives however much good you think you are doing. Of course Harvey's cheque will be very useful but I would rather have the debts than the letter that came with it. I hate Harvey to be angry and think badly of me; strange as it may seem I am very fond of him. If you don't realise this, then as Harvey has told *me*, you should not interfere when you don't know the facts.

Yours, Cornelia

Mrs Lamb to Harvey Lamb

Bede Street,
September 25th

Dear Harvey,

Thank you so much for the cheque. I am very glad to have it, although I know it doesn't mean that you have forgiven me. I suppose Peter Bath did not tell you that it was I who solved the mystery and got the whole thing cleared up; perhaps I can't take very much credit for it and in any case you would not want to hear about it from me. Anyway, it is over and I am back in Bede Street, and that is probably all you want to know.

Things are not very cheerful here as Spencer is married and there is no one among our poets who can take his place. There is a contender for it – one Cedric Fishtoft, who has none of the qualifications as he is neither good-looking nor polite and is known not to rhyme. Furthermore, he has had a volume of poetry published and rather well reviewed. It is called *The Crapyard* and its existence has so far been concealed from Aunt Lucy. I saw it reviewed in the T.L.S. and congratulated Fishtoft last time I saw him. He said, 'Yes. Don't tell the old lady,' so now I have Fishtoft in my power. This took place the night before last when we had the first poets' assembly since Spencer's defection. *The empty chair* was very much in evidence. The grade of Madeira was reduced and the sandwiches thinner on the plates. Up to now, Fishtoft has always refused to read anything of his own – and considering the title of his published work I am not surprised – and has been once or twice cruelly forced to read Alfred Austin or the more exuberant kinds of Browning. This time, however, he got up and read a truly atrocious piece of his own about a deserted loch and got a melancholy commendation for it from Aunt Lucy. It must have cost him something to write and read such a thing, and I suppose this spiritual outlay is designed to get a substantial return. If I liked him better I might tell him how very steep is the uphill row he has chosen to hoe. Aunt Lucy cannot understand how Percy (a limp young man who once got something into *Punch*) can bring such a monster into her drawing-room. So he is trying, so far as his natural limitations will allow, to ingratiate himself with Klara Meiss, our new reader, who can be no more to his taste than 'I must go down to the seas again'. But perhaps he feels that he must appear to appreciate both, if he is to get a firm foothold at court. You know how inexorably Aunt Lucy's acquaintances are divided into geese and swans – it is going to be entertaining to see whether Fishtoft manages to struggle out of one category into another.

I am leading a quiet life, as you see. I shall ring up one or two people soon and perhaps go out a bit; it ought to be easier to get away now that Klara Meiss is on the scene. She is here a good deal and always makes herself useful. Roylance Cowlinshaw calls her 'a dainty rogue in concrete', but I think that is rather unkind. Whatever her faults, at least she diverts a little of Aunt Lucy's attention from me.

She has just this moment knocked on my door and asked me what I am doing; so perhaps that last sentence was a little optimistic. Thank you once again for the cheque, I don't deserve it. But I don't think I deserve the letter you wrote with it either. It seems to suggest that I have done something awful, that can't be repaired. But nothing has *happened*, everything is still the same, isn't it? Do write to me again.

Yours, Cornelia

Mrs Nieman to Mrs Lamb

New York.
September 29th

Dear Cornelia,

Thank you for your condolences about Melville. I am taking the opportunity to change all the apartment furniture around, though, as Harvey says, it is rather Melville one wants to change. Just now I have a lot of visitors, girl-friends come to compare bad husbands, and Prudence comes up often in hopes to find Harvey. I have also friends of Adam's in town from Poland who must be shown the sights.

I have seen Tigran a few times since he got back. He got a job better than the one he left, so he says. First time I saw him, he came to borrow sheets as Angélique set fire to his apartment. She locked herself in the bedroom and piled some furnishings on the bed and set light to them with the diamond-encrusted lighter given her by the Prince. Lucky Tigran is strong and broke down the door before the firemen were needed. This morning Angélique called me to say she had sold her Cadillac and is buying Tigran a new bed, new drapes, new carpets and some statues, for his bedroom. It will be more punishment to live with Angélique's taste than a burned bed, I think he fears she will refurnish the whole apartment, now that she is so rich. The Prince is temporarily out of town.

It is hot here – I just had a letter from Melville's mother inviting us to Maine, which puts me in a difficulty. If he intends coming back, I do not want to start trouble in his family. I should like to go out of town, but I do not think I could support it alone.

I hope all goes well now with you. You should watch out for the German, she will depose you if she can.

Yours, Christiane

I had finished this letter but not sealed it when I received one from you. I am sorry you are angry with me but I do not know why you should suppose Harvey thinks badly of you. I do not think sending someone £500 shows this.

C.

Harvey Lamb to Mrs Bender New York. September 29th

Dear Aunt Lucy,

Do forgive me for being so negligent in my correspondence. The pressure of work here is very high and there is also, of course, the necessity, as part of my job, to lead an active and especially a varied social life. I do not believe in living in a country as a member of the foreign service and cultivating only one's fellow countrymen.

It is very good of you to write to me regularly with news of Cornelia. As you mentioned, I have had to write to her once or twice myself lately, but purely on business matters. I am afraid our normal communications are not yet restored.

I am sorry that you have not heard from Uncle Hugo but I am sure there is no need to worry about him. If he has gone into the interior we must not expect to hear much, and he will be with people who know the country and would avoid anything risky.

I am sorry to hear that you do not approve of Spencer's choice of a wife. I am sure that marriage will be an excellent thing for him, and perhaps the girl will improve (so far as you are concerned) with acquaintance. I always thought

Spencer a little lacking in drive, but perhaps with someone to provide for, he will improve in that direction! Give him my regards.

I am very comfortably settled now in a perfectly adequate apartment. New York is not quite so dangerous as you suppose, though it is in some ways an uncomfortable city to live in. It is interesting, however, and we are doing some good work here. I have made quite a number of friends and have found some helpful ladies who can deal with any domestic difficulties that arise. The Americans are, of course, immensely hospitable and one has to be very firm, otherwise one would never spend an evening at home. You would be amused to see my household – a black cook and a Puerto Rican boy I have taken on to do my valeting. Despite the complaints here about the quality of domestic service, they are doing very well and I have had several extremely successful dinner parties at which I persuaded Christiane Nieman (a friend, incidentally, of Cornelia's) to preside. It is not easy to repay the enormous amount of hospitality one receives, and I will not surrender to the ghastly institution of the cocktail party of which in any case one gets more than enough in official circles. But I think I am keeping my end up, in spite of having no wife to help me.

The weather here is somewhat oppressive, but I am intending to take a couple of weeks' leave and go up to New England where I hope to get some fishing.

Once again I must apologise for not replying to your letters sooner – I am appalled to find how long it is since I wrote to you. I will try to do better in the future and will hope to hear from you again soon.

Yours affectionately, Harvey

Mrs Lamb to Mrs Nash Bede Street.
October 5th

Darling Mary,

I had dinner with Margot and Murray Bassett last night and they told me that they had seen you while they were in Suffolk and that you are well (and looking very handsome, Murray said!). It was so nice to have news of you – I have been meaning to write to you for ages and tell you all about the drama of Tigran, in which after all you were in a way involved. But I am sure Margot saved me the trouble. I told *her* the whole story – well, I felt bound to considering that at various points in it I had borrowed her car and rather a lot of money – and although I naturally asked her not to tell anyone else, I know that her interpretation of a request of that sort is to tell everybody separately, and swear them all to secrecy. I expect you are relieved to know that your services as an alibi won't be needed any more. I suppose you think poor Tigran's stay in jail, and all the trouble, were a fitting penalty for our reprehensible behaviour; you are in a perfect position to say, 'I told you so.' All the same, the consequences were not so disastrous as they might have been. Everybody seems to have more or less settled down again, except Harvey. It is rather disconcerting, but for the first time in my life I feel that I don't really know what is in his mind, although he has behaved all through this business exactly as I would have expected him to do, even to the extent of perhaps falling in love with Christiane Nieman, to whom I consigned him in New York. I am not sure that he *has* done so, but there are several straws in the wind, with which I could make bricks, if I wanted to build something. One is, that Christiane passed on to Harvey something which I specifically asked her to keep to herself, thereby proving that her loyalty has moved from me to him. Then, Christiane knows not only that Harvey sent me a cheque to pay my debts, but the *amount*. As Harvey usually thinks of money as no more fit a subject of conversation than what they call 'biological functions', it proves how very far she is in his confidence. Aunt Lucy had a letter from him a day or two ago. She shook her head over it and said to me, 'Ah, Cornelia, he is giving dinner parties! You had better look out!' So perhaps I *had* better look out, especially as Christiane's husband has left her.

You will say that if it has happened you are not in the least surprised and that I deserve it. Do write to me, even so. I wish I could ask you to come and stay, but I am afraid Aunt Lucy would say she could not ask it of Mrs Lockett. It is useless to tell her that there would not be much extra work to do – Aunt Lucy thinks of the most undemanding guest as a kind of cosmic inspector whose first act will be to climb to the top of the china cupboard and test the curlicues of the Dresden tea set for dust. In any case I am afraid you are in Aunt Lucy's bad books for your constant demands for my company during the summer, for not having a telephone and for other deficiencies which I forget. *She* will forget them in time, and you will revert to your role of a deserving person. She has always pitied you for being married to someone who swears.

When I was in Paris I met by chance a young man called Charles Bellavance who I got to know on a boat coming back from America and who in fact constituted a *last straw*, according to Harvey. It is really extraordinary how these accidental encounters positively seem to encourage what they call irregular relationships. He is very young, rather solemn and very touchy. He is charming, none the less, and if Tigran and Harvey both get married, he is at present my only prospect. It is quite a pleasant one, so long as the vista does not extend too far; I cannot see myself spending long with someone who is insulted by mistakes in French grammar.

It occurs to me that I told Christiane that I had met M. Bellavance, which I suppose in effect means that I have told Harvey. I shall not be able to write to her as I used to. But as I am sure she only tells Harvey what she thinks is good for him, I suppose I ought to be content with that.

I hope all is well with you and the children.

Yours, Cornelia

Mrs Lamb to Tigran Leontyev Bede Street.
October 5th

Darling Tigran,

I am so sorry to hear that Angélique tried to burn your house down – it seems a poor return for those hours you spent with her parents, when you might have been enjoying yourself. Well, there are people who think that all pleasure should be paid for, and if they are right you can feel now that nothing is owing. *I* am getting out of the red by living with Aunt Lucy when I should prefer to be living with you, and mortifying the spirit, if not the flesh, by spending time with Klara Meiss. I told you about Klara Meiss, didn't I? (Do you remember when I told you? It was raining, and we lit a fire which smoked fearfully. We lay on the sofa and made toast. I shall always be fond of the taste of smoky toast, and I shall have some next time I am in a restaurant grand enough to give you *exactly* what you order.)

Aunt Lucy has been shopping a great deal lately which is a painful occupation for everyone concerned in it, except presumably herself. Her technique is of the period of Mr Kipps. She seats herself at the counter and expects things to be brought to her, most of which she greets with cries of 'Good gracious, no!' or '*Abominable!*' pronounced, for some reason, with a French accent. Even in the very best shops this method is not popular. In some of them our entrance is like that of the black-hats in a Western who empty the main street of the town as the population scurry indoors and close the shutters. I think she is throwing herself into an all-out campaign to get Spencer away from his wife. She bought four hats yesterday. One of them has a wing-span of about two foot six, so I hope she will be discreet when she wears it in the house and not go too near the Capodimonte. It was clearly built for a garden party, so it may be destined to play a part in the war against Mr Viot downstairs. He has quite unaccountably refused to have an extra key cut for his garden door for Aunt Lucy to use whenever she likes. Selfishness has now been nominated top vice in her list, a place held by Greed when preparing for the last dinner party, and Drunkenness when ordering Madeira for the poets. She has also bought a garden chair with a foot-rest and a canopy, which with the hat would almost fill Mr Viot's plot, or at least roof it in. I don't know when she is planning to deploy these weapons in their proper place. We have not been into the garden for some weeks; we can only look into it from above and note how seldom Mrs Viot herself sits there.

I have been obliged to tear myself away from these dramas from time to time in order to go to some very pleasant dinners and parties. At the last one I met a millionaire called Mr Mortleman to whom I became instantaneously devoted. He has a withdrawn, abstracted air, like a writer inhabiting his two worlds. I thought he was counting money in his head, but I was wrong. His fortune is past counting, and instead he occupies himself with large-scale and long-term jokes of a peculiarly quiet and unsensational kind. At this party he was as jubilant as so melancholy a man can be, because he had just been introduced to someone called Mr Piper, who played the flute. He at once bought him, cash down, to add to the orchestra he has at his country house. I was introduced to him just as the transaction was concluded and the flautist had gone away. 'I am passionately fond of music,' he said in a sad way, as though it was something he could not buy. Then he told me about his band, reciting their names with his sad eyes fixed on my face. Mr Bowyer, Mr Sawyer, Miss Fiedler, Mr Bangs, Mr Singer, Mr Player. . . . They were all professional musicians, and if they were not up to his standards he had them trained. 'It is taking me a long time,' he said, with the secretive relish of the obsessed collector. He had one failure only, with a Mrs Trumpet, who could not be persuaded, even on a part-time basis. The orchestra live in a wing of the house and play at meals, in the musicians' gallery. 'Mr Reader keeps them in order,' he said and added with modest pride that Mr Reader was his secretary. His accountant was Mr Teller, a rare one, that. The gardeners were easy: Green, Barrow. . . . I asked him how he managed it. 'Sometimes we advertise,' he said, sighing heavily. He had made one or two concessions; the manservant's *middle* name was Butler, called after Yeats.

'It's like Happy Families,' I said. He looked at me as though he had never heard those two words in conjunction before. Just as we parted he said he had not caught my name. When I told him, a very faint light seemed to come into his eyes and his moustache moved, almost in a smile. Perhaps he is thinking of starting a farm, or a zoo.

I have been interrupted by Aunt Lucy, who has lost her emerald brooch *again*, so I must finish this letter and join in the search. Do write to me. I have slightly quarrelled with Christiane, so I am not likely to get much news of you from her. I have not heard from Mary Nash since all the bother, but I expect she will forgive me in time. She can't help disapproving of people who are not as nice as she is. She disapproves of me *basically*, because she thinks that people without children have been enjoying the cheese without springing the trap. She was very kind, though, when you were here, wasn't she? She is a good girl.

Roylance Cowlinshaw sends his very warm regards. So would everyone else, if they knew how much you deserve them.

Much love, dear Tigran.

Your Cornelia

Mrs Nash to Mrs Lamb

Suffolk.
October 8th

Dear Cornelia,

Thank you for your letter. It was very nice seeing Margot and Murray, the first people other than locals that I have talked to for what seems years. Margot told me all about your Armenian and said it was all in the papers, but I do not have time to read the papers so I missed it. The children were very excited about the animal lovers' march to Downing Street which they saw on TV but, of course, I did not realise that it had anything to do with you. You were incredibly lucky that it ended as it did – I suppose it might easily have ruined Harvey's career. You really should not be surprised if he is angry with you, but I am sure he will not fall in love with Christiane Nieman, he is much too sensible. There is no need to start talking about marrying some Frenchman just because Harvey has had dinner with another woman. Not everybody is like you.

I can hardly believe that Harvey's Aunt Lucy still knows nothing about it all. I don't know how anyone could be so stupid, or so unsuspecting. With detectives actually coming to the house, so Margot told me, and so many people involved, I should have thought it was bound to come out in time. But perhaps you will have your usual luck and be able to keep it from her at least until you decide to leave her house.

I would love to come up and stay with you and I may propose myself one of these days if you can persuade your Aunt Lucy to have me. We are more than usually broke at the moment, however, so I don't think it is likely just yet. Besides, I have no clothes I could possibly wear in London, or anyway in Bede Street. Larry thinks this a fatuous reason for refusing to go anywhere, but then he thinks all women ought to dress like Dorelia. His leg is much better but he has started on a work which involves a lot of climbing ladders and lugging pieces of scrap metal about. It is too big for the studio so I am very much hoping he will finish it before the wet weather comes. Christopher says it looks like a collaboration between Reg Butler and Steptoe, which I think is rather good. Jeannie's baby was born in August, but she has not yet decided whether to marry her boy – he is himself a most indecisive youth and completely under her thumb. I wish they would marry but of course Larry disagrees and she is much more likely to take his advice than mine. It is nice to have a baby in the house again, especially now that all the family rows about it have died down. Aunt Betty tells me that we have been cut out of three different wills. Do you ever see any of the aunts these days? If you do, you might try to find out whether this is true. Not that it makes much difference. I can't imagine inheriting anything, any more than I can imagine having any money that is not earmarked for some necessity, and spent before it is received. Christopher is going to be an anthropologist, Elizabeth a nun, Daniel a sculptor and Jeannie I suppose has already started on a domestic life, so things are not likely to change. Larry says all well-paid work is contemptible and unfortunately this seems to be one of the few things he and the boys agree on. I can only hope they will change their minds in time.

My love to Murray and Margot, and to Harvey when next you write.

Yours, Mary

Mrs Nieman to Mrs Lamb New York.
October 10th

Dear Cornelia,

I heard from Melville. He is in Florida with Earl, working in a motel. Two qualified lawyers, stoking the central heating plant and cleaning windows. I think he told me all this not only to get sympathy but to annoy me, he knows how I hate waste. I think I probably divorce him. Harvey says wait and think about it, and this I do, but not for long, it seems an untidy way to live.

I see Tigran quite frequently and even more frequently Angélique who complains that although she completely renews his bedroom at her expense he will not sleep in it, or anyway not with her. He fills the apartment with guests but this is not unusual and is no excuse. Angélique accuses him of having an affair with Adam and with the man who delivered the statues she bought him. She thinks he learned such things in England. She still has the Arab prince who just bought her a horse. She says he is terribly jealous and at the moment she is naturally very frustrated as there is nobody for him to be jealous of. She asked me to invite them both to dinner, which I did, and she was very disappointed that they did not try to kill each other. Au contraire, the prince liked Tigran so well that he gave him his cigarette-case when he admired it. Angélique wore chiffon with no underclothes but nobody was impressed except perhaps Prudence Darnley. Tigran after all is used to it, the Prince seemed not to notice, and Adam's brother Jan who I asked to make up the party, has also seen Angélique en deshabille having stayed often with Tigran. Tigran devoted himself to Prudence, so, of course, *she* had a wonderful evening and said to me afterwards, à propos d'Angélique, that she thought men were put off by too much blatant sex appeal. She has none, so nice men are nice to her and she is lucky enough not to see why. I think now she transfers her affection to Tigran from Harvey which will be a relief. I am rather tired of her popping in to borrow things in the hope Harvey is here. She will borrow an iron, return it stone cold and say it 'saved her life' because her own iron was on the blink. I do not like these untruthful excuses. But she has not been up here since the dinner party except once, to ask for Tigran's telephone number which I gave her with pleasure. I suppose it might be that he finds her attractive, he is very tolerant in his tastes. For her, she has no shame whatever, she simply rushes at people as though she were a child. When I hint to her not to be quite so obvious, she says it is her nature. She is very pleased with herself, so I will not interfere, and perhaps one day she surprises me with a husband.

Now that I have more time I am taking a course in shorthand and typing, so I am ready to earn my own living if need be. I do not think Melville cheats me over the alimony, but one never can be sure. As Harvey says, it is good to have a second line of defence.

I hope all goes well with you.

Yours, Christiane

Tigran Leontyev to Mrs Lamb

New York.
October 15th

Darling Cornelia,

Thank you very much for your letters, lovely to know that you are well and happy and having fun. I am too, I have wonderful new job, earning plenty of money which I save up to come back to England soon and see you. Thank you for postcard of Mr Landseer, I put it on my shelf in place of honour and keep it there for ever. Whenever I see it it reminds me of wonderful times we had together.

I go to Christiane's apartment sometimes to talk about you. Last time I met your husband there, he is very nice bloke. Christiane is very well, looking very good. Her husband left her which is rather pity. Perhaps Adam comes back to her, he is alone too. Perhaps I take him with me next time I go to see her.

No news, darling princess. Do write again, I like to know what you are doing and love your nice long letters.

Love and kisses,

Your Tigran

Mrs Lamb to Mrs Nieman

Bede Street.
October 20th

Dear Christiane,

You will be glad to hear that I have forgiven you your breaches of confidence; mainly because I am dying to know how Tigran and Harvey got on when they met at your apartment. Everything relevant seems to be happening in New York and though Tigran writes charming letters they do not exactly tell me anything. As Madame de Stael says, speech is not his language, or at any rate writing is not.

I am sorry you are having so much trouble with Angélique. Do tell her from me that there is a very simple reason for his not wanting to sleep with her in his new bed – it is that he does not love her any more. I am sure she should marry the Eastern potentate, they sound well suited and he would certainly recommend himself to Madame Mouscadet, who, according to Tigran, is simply besotted about money. They could all live happily ever after in the house in Paris which has room for several Eastern caravans, and the horse could live in the courtyard.

I dined last night with Margot and Murray – they have been in the country and had spent a day with the Nashes. Margot said she had a long confidential conversation with Mary about me, which she related to me in great detail. Margot really is invaluable; without her one would never really know one's friends' opinions, and as they have always been expressed under the strictest secrecy one can rely on their being authentic. Mary's theory is that I am tremendously insecure and that is why I have affairs with people. I can't understand why as soon as anybody does anything that gives them pleasure it is supposed to be a *sign* of something. Fat women eating cream buns, tycoons snug in the bar, me and Tigran, I suppose – we are all assumed to be clinging to some frightening psychological brink, rather than just doing something we like doing. I should have thought it would be more insecure *not* to do as one liked; but Mary once started a course in social psychology, so that would be too simple for her. She is convinced that there are what she calls cross-currents and that I am swirling about in them more or less haphazard, so that my ultimate landfall is completely unpredictable. She thinks I am immature; but perhaps that is something one grows out of.

If I were younger, the prospect might be brighter; I feel I really have not time to develop into the character Mary thinks I ought to be. Margot said it was twaddle, but she is interested in what people do and not why they do it.

Life in Bede Street is overcast. Aunt Lucy has been forcing me to read to her a particularly gruesome work about missionaries and has become convinced that Uncle Hugo has been killed and his brain eaten to raise the I.Q. of some savage man. I am trying to find a book about Zambia as an antidote, because I have so far not been able to convince her on my own account that they have civil servants, telephones and skyscrapers. We have heard nothing from Uncle Hugo, but it is useless to remind her of his failings as a correspondent; he has suddenly become her poor little brother, the only one she had left. The episode of the woodworm has been forgotten, and also another even more heinous legacy which Uncle Hugo left behind; something to do with the lavatory, too vulgar to be explained in any detail. Mrs Lockett would only tell me that one day when Aunt Lucy rose from it 'everything was blue' and that this resulted in expensive and, as it turned out, embarrassing visits first from Dr Dench and then from the plumber, who said it was the most unusual thing he had ever had to deal with. This was all kept from me at the time and even Mrs Lockett did not know the whole story because Aunt Lucy bravely dealt with it herself, in the reputable tradition of shielding the servants from the unpleasant side of life, so far as possible. I don't know what drove poor Uncle Hugo to take these complicated revenges. I suppose they are just manifestations of the exquisite pleasure he and Aunt Lucy seem to find in tormenting each other. At the moment, however, they might never have taken place; we are mourning him, prematurely I am certain. Aunt Lucy has found a speckled photograph of him in a sailor suit, for her dressing-table; and Poor Maud has been asked to lunch, to add fuel to the pyre. Her repertoire luckily contains several appropriate reminiscences: a whole party of acquaintances of her grandfather were eaten in Brazil ('Of all places!' Aunt Lucy said). They included a General, which added piquancy to the story, and perhaps to the savage feast as well.

Aunt Lucy is always cheered by lunch with Poor Maud. It is encouraging to think that one has been spared the dreadful fates which overtake so many decent people. Poor Maud's victims never deserve their ends. 'Such a nice man too!' she says with the satisfaction of proving once again the cruelty of fate. Mrs Lockett does not approve. 'Ooh, I think it's morbid,' she said to me afterwards, having brought in the pudding in time to hear about the man who was run over twice, by his own wife. She had to admit, though, that Poor Maud's visit left an afterglow that lasted until the six o'clock news, which is always expected to contain some Zambian disaster, and seems a disappointment when it does not.

Write to me.

Yours, Cornelia

Mrs Bender to Harvey Lamb

Bede Street.
October 21st

My dear Harvey,

I write to you with a heavy heart, for I am desperately anxious about Hugo, from whom I have still heard nothing. I have the most dreadful premonitions – he is so careless of his own safety, and he was far from well when he set out on this mad journey. I am so sorry to worry you, dear, when you have troubles of your own, but I wondered whether there was any enquiry you could make that would set our minds at rest. Women are so helpless in these things. I think Cornelia feels as I do, for it was she who suggested I should write to you. Even in the midst of my anxiety I could feel pleasure at this, because it shows how much she relies on you and I am sure wishes you were here to help us. Since she has been back from Wood Cottage she has been quiet, perhaps a little sad. I have noticed that you have not written to her lately and I have heard her asking Mrs Lockett whether there are any letters for her, so I am sure she misses you and feels the separation.

I am so glad to hear from your last letter that you have a nice flat and adequate staff. I think you may well have chosen them wisely, even if it seems a little strange to you. Grandfather always used to say, when he came back from Khartoum, that your black makes the best servant if he is well trained and strictly dealt with. I am sure you have enough of grandfather in you to follow his advice. I am glad you are making friends, but I should not take these friendships too seriously. Your dear father used to say the Americans were friendly with everybody, which does not show very much discrimination. I hope there are some pleasant people at our Embassy so that you can have a change from American hospitality. It is a country of extremes, which does not suit the calm English temperament, but I hope you are not finding it too trying. I am sure you will be a success there and will be rewarded with a job in a more simpatico country.

It is kind of you to send your regards to Spencer. I have seen him only once since the débâcle. I have not had the heart to entertain recently, without news of Hugo, and feeling that the blow may fall at any moment. A further difficulty is that Mr Viot has begun to behave in a most extraordinary way, I am beginning to wonder whether he is quite sane and I do not know whether it is wise to ask anyone to the house, in case he may do them some mischief as they pass his door. I have complained to the landlord, who is usually a most reasonable person, but on this he is not helpful. As you see, we are having more than our fair share of disasters at the moment, so I will not burden you with any more. It would be the greatest comfort to me if you could make some enquiries about poor Hugo – you, after all, are in the thick of things there, and I am sure you will be able to take steps that would be quite beyond me.

Bless you my dear boy,

Your affectionate aunt, Lucy

Harvey Lamb to Mrs Bender New York.
October 29th

Dear Aunt Lucy,

I am sorry that you are worried about Uncle Hugo. I have sent a signal to our man in Lusaka and I am sure we shall have some news of him soon. Please forgive the delay in replying – I have only just got back from a fortnight in Maine, and found your letter waiting for me. However, I got busy at once and will let you know the moment I have anything to report. In the meantime, please do not be anxious. You have often said yourself what a bad correspondent Uncle Hugo can be, and I expect communications there are not of the best in any case.

I have had an excellent holiday and have come back feeling very fit. I stayed with some delightful people and got some fishing. I have come back of course to a mountain of work, but it is interesting, and I should not like to be in New York with too much time on my hands.

I am so sorry you are having trouble with your neighbours. Viot has always seemed to me a curious chap, but I don't think you need fear violence from him. Try a little charm with him, I am sure you can heal the breach if you choose, and it is never a good idea to be on bad terms with your neighbours. They have so much opportunity to make themselves a nuisance!

Please do not speak of 'burdening me with your troubles.' I am only too pleased to be of any help I can – it would be a poor do if I could not occasionally help my favourite aunt! As for adding to my troubles, you need not worry, as I have none that will not sort themselves out in time.

I hope Cornelia is well. Please give her my love. I will write to you again directly.

Yours affectionately, Harvey

Mrs Lamb to Mrs Nash

Bede Street.
November 2nd

Darling Mary,

I have retreated into my little room much against Aunt Lucy's will. Her passion for constant human companionship is even more unbridled since she became convinced that Uncle Hugo has been eaten in Zambia. Also, a state of hostility exists between us and Mr Viot downstairs, and plans for his destruction have to be laid without a moment to lose. These two subjects, equally fervid, have been discussed during the past few days to the absolute exclusion of anything else, and my concern for them is beginning to wane. The story of Uncle Hugo's saintly childhood, wayward youth and brilliant adulthood gets longer and more detailed with each telling. It has gone down very well with Klara Meiss, who naturally takes the apocalyptic view: that saints' lives end in martyrdom. At first, she was the victim of a misunderstanding owing, I suppose, to Aunt Lucy's misty way of speaking and her own imperfect grasp of English – she thought Uncle Hugo was positively dead, and I don't think she has ever recovered from the conviction. I take the opposite view that one only has to get through today and a letter will arrive from him tomorrow. Aunt Lucy makes brave attempts to agree with me, but then says with a melancholy smile that something tells her that poor Klara is right. She can be distracted from gloomy prophecies only by her other preoccupation – Mr Viot's villainy, and on that subject too the seam has been well worked. After all, we don't know Mr Viot very well and most of his sins and vices can only be suspected. Plans for upsetting him or driving him out of the house offer more scope. In this I have been much more helpful than Klara, who is inhibited by her respect for the law. I thought of some brilliant things, such as introducing snakes under the door, but I rather like Mr Viot, and I have had to moderate my suggestions since I heard Aunt Lucy ringing up Harrods to ask the price of snakes. Mr Viot's claim to our enmity began by his refusal to give Aunt Lucy a key to the garden which belongs to his flat but which *she* thinks should be shared by us all. This convicted him of obstinacy and selfishness, but now he has become 'difficult' as well. Poor Mrs Viot, perhaps to counteract some irritation inherent in living with Mr V, has started to do the pools. Aunt Lucy has always considered pools vulgar and therefore destroys buff envelopes from Liverpool with their telltale special markings, whenever she sees them. She is dedicated to keeping our hall table free of such plebeian things and regularly tears up all advertising material that she sees there, and sometimes confiscates magazines or catalogues of which she does not approve. I don't know how the Viots discovered what was happening to their weekly forms, but when confronted, Aunt Lucy did not deny it. She said that they littered up the place and looked common. Apparently Mr Viot could not be made to agree from the aesthetic point of view, or even from the practical one; he showed himself to be not only obstinate but selfish and grasping. After all, as Aunt Lucy pointed out, Mrs Viot does not *need* to do the pools. I think she implied that it was taking bread out of the mouths of the poorer classes. But Mr V. was most unreasonable, and has since sent us several angry notes, asking her to stop 'tampering with the mails'. Mrs Lockett wonders where it will all end. *I* am sure that it will not end at all, so long as Mr Viot can fill the vacancy left by the canonisation of Uncle Hugo.

Since I last wrote to you I have had news of Harvey. He worte a letter to Aunt Lucy which for once she let me read. He sounded astonishingly cheerful. I am glad of it, of course, but it does rather confirm my feeling that he has fallen in love with Christiane, specially as he has just spent a fortnight in Maine, which is where her parents-in-law live, and where she said she was thinking of going herself. Perhaps they went there together. There seemed to be a certain complacency between the lines. He said he had no troubles that could not be sorted out and mentioned me in the next sentence. It is nice to think of him having a good time, but I hope he will not get too serious. Though come to think of it, Christiane would suit him very nicely. I know you won't agree with this. But at any rate, I promise you that I will not marry M. Bellavance, whatever happens.

Yours, Cornelia

Mrs Lamb to Harvey Lamb

Bede Street.
November 5th

My dear Harvey,

I read your last letter to Aunt Lucy and was glad that you sounded so cheerful. It is more than we are here: the absence of Uncle Hugo and the presence of Mr Viot are keeping our tragedy level high. When it threatens to sag we think about Christmas Dinner. Major Markette and poor Roylance were booked in October, as though they were social butterflies who must be caught before other eager hostesses could get their nets out. Spencer was precluded by his marriage, and will join those who qualify for the pathetic toast of absent friends. Only three weeks ago Aunt Lucy was saying that no one could take his place. But today she announced that someone had done so, and a most unlikely candidate: Fishtoft, of all people. I can't think how he has done it. It is true that at the past Penny Reading he produced one about an English country lane which outdid everything in what Aunt Lucy calls simplicity. Then he outstayed everyone, and afterwards Aunt Lucy remarked that the poor young man had had a hard life. But he cannot have done it on pity alone – his poverty is not picturesque and I can't imagine his being able to express gratitude gracefully. But there it is – he is a candidate for one-sixth of the Christmas duck. Mrs Lockett is not so surprised as I. She says Aunt Lucy has been giving him money. I didn't believe it but Mrs Lockett says that after the last party she went out and looked down the well of the stairs and saw Fishtoft at the bottom, counting pound notes. There were only three of them so no great harm is done but it is rather strange. I do not like Fishtoft, but I would not say he was cut out to be a sponge. Do you think I ought to defend Aunt Lucy from these potential parasites? Those of Major Markette's generation have been on the scene for so long that one feels that they are part of the running expenses, and anyway their demands are modest. Fishtoft, once he got into his stride, might well become a major liability – although I suppose he is only taking the place of Spencer, who must have been quite costly when he was the favourite. Trips to the bank fell in frequency dramatically after his defection but have just risen again, with nothing very much to show for it. I think Klara Meiss too might be expecting a little share. She asked Mrs Lockett not very long ago how much Aunt Lucy was worth – not in so many words, but her intention was clear. She got, as Mrs Lockett said, 'a short shift' and is none the wiser, but it confirms my doubts that anyone, however saintly, could consider the Forsyte Saga, historical romances and Lamb family history their own reward. Mrs Lockett said vigorously 'that young woman gets up my nose' – and I don't think it is only Klara's increasingly proprietorial manner towards the china cupboard and the larder; she believes that Klara has *hopes*, and does not think she deserves them. I don't suppose any of this matters very much – after all, Aunt Lucy is one of those people whose financial well has mysterious springs which somehow fill it up however often the bucket is let down, and goodness knows she economises rigorously enough in some directions. She has taken recently to counting the number of tomatoes and apples in a pound, so that each individual one can be the subject of amazement and indignation. She applied the same test to Brussels sprouts, but the results were not so sensational, and to Mrs Lockett's relief that particular piece of accountancy was discontinued.

Apart from playing my appointed role in these domestic dramas, I am leading a fairly quiet life, though I dined recently with Murray and Margot, and have been to two sedate supper parties, suitable to my position as a grass widow. I am still looking for a flat, but the only pretty ones are not grand enough for *you*, and the grand ones are all

rather excessive. The last one I saw had a huge rectangular drawing-room with two vast chandeliers so high up as to be almost out of sight. The effect was exactly like that place in Vienna where they make those unfortunate horses do the twostep. If we lived there, I would have to get the fire brigade in once a year to clean the crystals. There seem to be snags like this in every flat I look at, which I suppose is only evidence of some atavistic hatred of change. Looking through empty rooms is quite an agreeable occupation, however, so I shall go on doing so in a leisurely manner, in spite of Aunt Lucy's disapproval. When I come back from one of these expeditions, she always makes some reference to my 'poor little room' and receives my descriptions with that tactful silence which as you know reproaches louder than words. I am of course committed to Christmas here, but after that I shall apply myself to the business with more energy. After all, I have been here eight months, and even Aunt Lucy couldn't accuse me now of what she calls 'rushing away'.

Well, Harvey, what are *you* doing? I heard not long ago from Christiane but she did not say much about you. I hope you are well and enjoying yourself as best you can among all those dreadful Americans with guns. It would be nice to hear from you.

Love, Cornelia

Mrs Nieman to Mrs Lamb New York.
November 7th

Dear Cornelia,

It is quite true that Tigran met Harvey here, but it was not on purpose. Tigran and Adam came unexpectedly and I could not prevent it. Harvey was so nice that at first I think he does not know who Tigran is; then I realise it is the calm British way of hiding the feelings. They talk quite a lot together, mostly about the war, and seem perfectly amicable.

I am rather worried about Harvey. I suppose you know that your débâcle with Tigran has caused him trouble here, and though you are out of the woods, he is not. He said to me last night, things look a little tricky, and you know he always minimises. I only hope the harm is not incurable, he does not deserve it.

I have more news of Melville. Friends of mine who were in Florida stayed at the motel where he works, and say they think he will soon get the sack, because he and Earl Custance are all the time quarrelling, especially when they clean windows. They make faces at each other through the glass. Reconciliations are worse. I don't think it is unlawful in America but it is unpopular and already some men threatened to beat him up. Melville does not like trouble so I think he may come back quite soon. Meantime, Adam comes to see me, twice in the past week. I try to cook him a nasty dinner, not to encourage him, but cannot do it, and he has a very comfortable evening talking about his marriage problems. He is staying now at Tigran's apartment and says he is lonely. I do not know how this can be, as there are never less than eight people there at any time of the day or night.

I am having visits again from Prudence Darnley, now to talk of Tigran instead of Harvey. She wishes to marry Tigran and asks my advice how to set about it. I tell her many others have thought of it but have not succeeded, which seems to encourage her. I do not want to do this as she is a nice girl really. Conversations are long because she does not say plainly what she means. Yesterday she asked me whether she should 'go the whole hog' with Tigran, a distasteful expression I never heard before and she had to translate it. It is bizarre, that she is verbally so coy when her manner is so shameless. I ask Tigran what he thinks of her and he laughs and says she is a very nice girl. He has no girl friend at the moment but even so I do not believe poor Prudence gets her hog.

I am so sorry your Aunt Lucy is worried about her brother. Harvey is making enquiries and I am sure he finds something out soon. He says there are no cannibals in Zambia. He is not worried himself, and he is fond of his uncle, so I think that is a good sign. He writes to his aunt again as soon as he has news.

Yours, Christiane

Harvey Lamb to Mrs Lamb New York.
November 9th

Dear Cornelia,

I am being recalled to London and shall be staying at Brown's Hotel from Tuesday the 13th. There is something of great importance that I want to discuss with you and I will telephone you as soon as I arrive. I hope you will be able to dine with me on Tuesday evening.

Yours, Harvey

Mrs Lamb to Mrs Nash Bede Street.
November 14th

Darling Mary,

The most extraordinary things are happening – Harvey is here! And guess what he's come for – to find out whether I love him! That's not quite how he put it, but it is what it amounts to. The old fox has got a girl friend in America – not Christiane but somebody we've never heard of. She is a sad figure, very young but divorced with two children. Her name is Nan, and Harvey is, as he puts it, emotionally involved with her, to the degree that he feels he ought to ask her to marry him. But being Harvey, he wanted to ask me first.

All this incredible information was imparted to me in a restaurant, a most un-Harvey-like procedure. He had not intended this – we were to dine, and then go back to the hotel and talk, but though I could have borne the suspense through three courses, apparently Harvey could not. I would have known he had something very important to say even if he had not written to tell me so, because his attitude towards me was so peculiar. He gave me a very chaste kiss, keeping a table between us so it was difficult to hug him, he said, 'How pretty you're looking' in an anguished sort of voice, and I caught him several times giving me that forbidden-fruit look one sometimes sees on the faces of nice men. Before we had finished the smoked salmon he had embarked on the subject of this Nan. He is clearly besotted about her and so was I by the time he had finished, in that odd way one is, about people who are loved by those one loves oneself. I advised him not to do anything rash, which is rather a reversal of the natural order of things. Then he asked me what my feelings were about him and about our marriage, and without really giving me time to answer he started a long dissertation on marriage in general, how women saw it as a stable institution but men saw all the flaws; I said that women saw the ceilings and for some reason it made him very angry. He got up (before he had even finished his coffee) and said I had never been able to take anything seriously. He would not let me go back to Brown's with him, he would not talk any more. So perhaps I have ruined my case, like Oscar Wilde, by making a bad joke. I do admit that I have a case; I don't want Harvey to marry this Nan. I do not want to let him go. I feel rather meek, in this situation, especially as Harvey has changed, rather alarmingly, for the better. He was looking very handsome, sunburned, and wearing a quite unorthodox suit. And when I told him I thought he had fallen in love with Christiane, he seemed surprised. He said that he liked and admired her; and in the course of his telling me about all her virtues, I got the distinct impression that she was not pretty enough for him. The same applied, with more force, to Prudence Darnley, an English girl who I had rather thought of as a nice safe fling for him to have, without side-effects. He referred to her, with damning firmness, as a very nice girl. So you see he has become discriminating, self-confident and perhaps a little more pleased with himself than he used to be. *You* will say that you are not surprised, and that I brought it on myself. Christiane would agree with you. I must say I do feel a little indignant with *her*; she must have known about this girl of Harvey's and yet she never gave me the slightest hint of it. She confined herself to disapproving remarks about me and Tigran, which seems to me very unfair. I wish I had kept all her letters, though. I believe there were hints about Harvey 'looking elsewhere' as they say, if I constantly set him the example. So I can't say I have not been warned. Even Aunt Lucy said I had better look out. *She* knows nothing about Harvey being here – he wants to get things ironed out, as he puts it, before confronting her. This is in itself extremely unlike Harvey, who has never in his life had anything to hide.

Apart from all this, Harvey brought mysterious news about Uncle Hugo. Apparently he has completely disappeared from Zambia. He had been in Lusaka, according to Harvey's man there, and some more far-flung places as well, but for the past weeks nobody has been able to find any trace of him. Harvey regards this as peculiar rather than worrying. I am not to say anything to Aunt Lucy until Harvey tells me. Luckily, Christmas is absorbing some of the attention which was being lavished exclusively on Uncle Hugo's memory. We have lists now, and have opened the groaning bottom drawer which contains the little things picked up at different times and awaiting allocation. Some of them have been there for several years, as being unsuitable to anybody at all. I suppose she feels that in another year she may have acquired new friends, with different tastes. The attack on Regent Street is plotted, but there is also to be a raid on Woolworths this year, for some *amusing little things*. I wish I could force Klara Meiss to go over the top in my place.

I have not heard from Harvey today. I rang him twice at his hotel but he was not there. I wonder what he is doing. It seems rather a waste, if he is only to be here a week, to spend the whole day without seeing each other, and he said nothing about our meeting tonight.

Mrs Lockett has just been in, sent by Aunt Lucy to ask whether I have seen her emerald-green umbrella. When she finds it, she will be armed for her assault on the Gift Departments; it is of peculiar strength and has been used to thrust into a shop door, which was closing at what Aunt Lucy considered an unreasonably early hour. The handle can be used to lasso fleeing shopmen, and the ferrule can be pointed and tapped like the stave of an irate lantern-lecturer. I hope I have an opportunity of telling Harvey how I shall be spending tomorrow, while he is gadding about London. Surely he will see that heroism ought to be rewarded.

My love to Larry and the children.

Yours, Cornelia

Mrs Bender to Harvey Lamb

Bede Street.
November 16th

My dear Harvey,

Even in the midst of my own troubles I am not neglecting to keep an eye on Cornelia, and I am afraid I have something rather unpleasant to tell you. She has been out for dinner for the past three evenings, giving Mrs Lockett almost no notice, and has been very reluctant to talk about it afterwards. And last night she spent at Mr and Mrs Bassett's, although she had not told me that she intended to do so. When she got back this morning she said the party broke up very late, and when she could not get a taxi, she was invited to stay. I am bound to tell you that I do not think she was telling me the whole truth. There was something evasive in her manner. I am very quick to feel such things. Of course I would not press her, she is a grown woman after all, but I felt I must tell you at once. I have thought for some time that she spends too much time with the Bassetts. They are continually giving parties, and as you know most of their friends are newspapermen and people of that kind. I know you saw a good deal of them when you were at home, but it is a different matter if Cornelia goes there alone. I do not want to worry you, when you are working so hard and in such difficult circumstances, but I wonder whether perhaps your policy of not writing to Cornelia is a good one – would it not be wiser to let her know occasionally that you are still her husband and that eventually (as I hope) you will be together again? I think a firm and friendly letter would not be out of place – but you will know best.

I have been longing to hear from you about Hugo, and I

hope you will let me know immediately, *whatever* the news may be. It is so dreadful to think of a splendid life like his ending in a question mark – anything would be better than that. Christmas will indeed be a miserable feast. I shall miss him every minute of the festivities. He was always the centre of the jolly Christmases we had at home.

I called Cornelia into the room a few moments ago to tell her I was writing to you and to ask if she had any message. She seemed confused and said she had none, but then added that of course she sent her love. She seemed for some reason surprised to know that I was writing to you. I am sure she is in some sort of difficulty. It is a pity she is not a confiding person, it would make things so much easier.

I shall not be able to write to you for a little while, as Christmas is upon us. But I shall be waiting every day for news from you that will end this dreadful suspense. I hope you will have as pleasant a Christmas as is possible for you, away from old England.

Your affectionate aunt, Lucy

Mrs Lamb to Mrs Nieman Bede Street.
November 16th

Darling Christiane,

You really are extraordinary! There was Harvey carrying on with this Nan and you never told me a word of it. I do think you might have given me just a hint. But I suppose you promised him you would not tell me, and I suppose your loyalty goes to the one you feel is most worthy of it. I forgive you, though; I am in a forgiving mood.

Poor Harvey – his fact-finding mission on our marriage has not gone according to plan. The first time we met we quarrelled, the second time we somehow ended up dancing in a rather riotous restaurant, and last night we spent together at Brown's Hotel. Now Harvey feels he has been unfaithful to Nan and is at any rate *pretending* to be very cut up about it. I think in fact he is feeling rather pleased with himself, he certainly looked it at breakfast this morning.

There are, however, as Sherlock Holmes would say, *deeper waters*, and I am afraid poor Harvey may well be in them up to his neck; I am trying very hard to think how to preserve him from total immersion. Apparently he did not come dashing over here to talk to me about Nan, or at least that was not his primary purpose. He was recalled, and is going to be grilled, like a poor old sausage, by the Security Services. It seems that this business of Tigran is still bothering people. His mysterious brother, who you told me had disappeared, is apparently alive and well and earning a good living as a spy in East Berlin. This seems to me to be beside the point, but Harvey is quite saintly about these wretched security people and says he can see their point of view. I can't, but I wasn't going to quarrel with him about it, he has quite enough to put up with. Apparently he has already had one nasty interview and is in for several more. He said nothing about this until last night; perhaps the shock of finding himself in bed with me again broke his resolve. He does seem to have changed a good deal since last I saw him – he has always been one of those people who would go to the stake rather than tell something he shouldn't. Perhaps being in bed with someone is more likely to make one talk than being all alone at the stake; anyway, I am very glad he is not going through all this without telling me. He is very anxious to keep it from Aunt Lucy and in fact has forbidden me to tell her that he is here. Such is my subservience to the man that when I tiptoed in this morning at eleven o'clock and unexpectedly found her up and waiting for me, I said I had been at Margot Bassett's. She exuded disbelief but, as is her way, did not express it. Later, however, she told me that she was writing to 'poor Harvey' and asked in a meaning manner whether I had any message. I shall have to try to intercept the letter and re-direct it to Brown's Hotel.

Dear Christiane, you have no idea how nice it is to be able to write to you without reserve. For some time now I have felt that I must watch what I was saying to you – a most unnatural state of affairs, brought on by my feeling that you were so much in Harvey's confidence; and *then* there were things I didn't want him to know. I also thought perhaps that he was in love with you, and even that he might step into Melville's shoes.

I have just been struck, this moment, by the horrible thought that *you* might be in love with *him*. You do mention him rather often in your letters. I hope very much not. I want all of us to be happy. I am so much so myself, that I would *give* you Harvey if I could. But I hope you don't want him – do write to me immediately and reassure me that you don't.

Yours, Cornelia

PS.—Everything I have told you about Harvey and his Security is *absolutely secret*, so you had better eat this letter when you have read it.

Mrs Lamb to Tigran Leontyev Brown's Hotel.
November 16th

Darling Tigran,

I have some extraordinary news for you – your brother has turned up in East Berlin! I don't know his exact address, and I am afraid that in any case the news is not all good: according to the Security Services, who discovered him, he is a spy, though on whose side I am not quite clear. Harvey told me all this only last night, and though I am very glad for your sake, it does make things rather complicated for us. People like Harvey are not supposed to have ever met anybody not absolutely aseptic, and the fact that he didn't even know your brother existed isn't the sort of thing Security Services take into account. They have brought poor Harvey home and although he doesn't say much, I can see he is worried. Don't tell anybody about this will you, darling, as it is supposed to be very hush-hush; but I thought, things being what they are, nobody would think to tell you, unless I did.

This is a very hasty note – Harvey will be in soon and I don't want him to know, at this moment, that I am writing to you. I will let you know developments soon.

Yours with love, Cornelia

Mrs Nash to Mrs Lamb

Suffolk.
November 17th

Dear Cornelia,

Thank you so much for your letter – I am sorry I did not have time to answer your earlier one, but we have been very busy here – Larry has got an exhibition! It is all very exciting – it will be opening just after Christmas, and of course there is a great deal to do beforehand. His only anxiety is whether his new work will be rusty enough by then. Unfortunately, he went away for a short break when he had completed it, and Daniel, trying to be helpful, threw a tarpaulin over it to protect it from the weather. Larry was furious when he got home and banged about for days. Now he goes and looks at it every morning and prays for rain, as though it were a prize dahlia. There is also a problem about whether it will go into the gallery. Larry wants it to stand on the pavement in Cork Street, but we don't know yet whether that will be possible. We shall have to have a crane, and a very large lorry. I do not know who is going to pay for it all, but I dare not mention such mundane matters just now. At any rate, one pleasant feature of the whole thing is that we shall be coming up to London some time fairly soon, though I do not know where we are all going to stay. Larry does not consider the problem of where one spends the night as any different from where one spends the day and says that in London there is plenty to do all round the clock to keep one occupied. If you have any ideas, I should be very grateful. It is quite possible that Larry has in fact made some arrangements, but even so it may be just as well to have something to fall back on.

I am so sorry to hear about your troubles with Harvey though you are right in thinking I am not surprised. He has been very patient for a long time – but I mustn't rub it in. Perhaps if you could persuade him to stay in England for a little while he might forget about the girl in America – though that does not seem very fair to her. You ought to think seriously about what you want. You are lucky to have a choice – a lot of people would give their eyes to be able to stop in the middle of a marriage and decide whether to go on with it or not. Perhaps you value yours more than you seem to – you have certainly exposed it to as many hazards as possible. But I suppose with your usual luck everything will work out for you. I hope it does, even if you don't deserve it.

I am sorry to hear about your Uncle Hugo. I know you were fond of him and I expect you are more worried than you seem. Don't you think he may be in hospital somewhere in Zambia? I think you told me he was over 80 and he may very well have been taken ill. I suppose Harvey has thought of that. I hope you will have some good news soon.

I will let you know our plans as soon as they are settled. You have no idea how much I am looking forward to being in London again!

Please give my love to Harvey if you see him.

Yours, Mary

Mrs Nieman to Mrs Lamb New York.
November 21st

Dear Cornelia,

You ask me to write immediately so I do it, to tell you I am not in love with Harvey though I think him one of the nicest men I ever met. I said nothing to you about Nan because Harvey asks me not to. She is a pretty woman left by an insurance man with two children and appeals to Harvey's sympathy. She is not so sad and helpless as she pretends which is not good, but one cannot blame her when she had the chance of such a husband. That chance looks less good now that you have seduced Harvey back but you should not be too sure of him, he has had a shock. He told me something of his security troubles, but not about the brother. I am not very surprised. In spite of being such a well-bred family they are not reliable.

Angélique is back in town and at a party at Tigran's offered the guests ten dollars each to go away, to be left alone with him, whether to make love or kill him was not clear. All went except Adam in case it was the latter, then she took all her clothes off, and then opened the window and screamed, but in New York nobody takes notice of such things. In the end she puts a fur coat over her nudity and goes downstairs saying she will sleep with the janitor. Adam says she is very pretty without clothes but a nuisance and thinks of cabling the Prince to come and take her away. Perhaps the harem would be a good place for her but it does seem a great waste that the Mouscadet fortune should go to the Prince who has one of his own.

I have strange news of Melville. A friend wrote that she met Earl Custance in Miami, bowed down with jewellery, coming out of a very expensive shop. He said Melville had come into money, but when she suggested they should all get together he was very evasive, would not tell her where they were staying, promised to call her but did not do so. She thinks I should worry about this, she says Earl may be very charming but one cannot trust that sort because they have no morals. I do not agree. Earl is very bien élevé and would certainly have the sense not to murder. I cannot think of any money Melville is likely to inherit except from his father, who I saw last week. I hope he has not taken up crime. It would not be his métier. I cannot write to give him advice as I do not know where he is. Prudence Darnley thinks this terrible. She says even if he was dead I would want to know the spot he is buried. She seems to be in a sombre mood.

I hope Harvey's troubles are soon over. Please give him my love.

Yours, Christiane

Mrs Lamb to Mrs Nieman Brown's Hotel.
November 28th

Darling Christiane,

The house in Bede Street is rocking under a storm of sensational trivialities, which necessitates my constant presence on the bridge beside the captain, who has innumerable domestic whirlpools and shallows to contend with, not to mention the jagged reefs of Christmas ahead. So although I am supposed to be settled here at Brown's with Harvey, I seem to be spending more time with Aunt Lucy than with him.

The first unsettling incident was the rediscovery of Uncle Hugo – not as picked bones in a Zambian jungle but at Pigpound Lane where he belongs. This extraordinary revelation of the obvious was made by Pansy Sapling, who had to come to London to see the Prime Minister about the importation of live alligators, and dropped in to see me on her way back from Downing Street. Apparently Uncle Hugo has been back for a fortnight, and the reason his movements could not be traced was that he had been brought home in the private plane of a Zambian millionaire who he had made friends with on the trip. Pansy says he has embarked on an enormous book which is going to take three years to write and will necessitate several more trips to Zambia and probably the Ivory Coast as well, and that this dusky Getty has put his plane at Uncle Hugo's disposal. Luckily Aunt Lucy was out when Pansy came. She had gone with Klara Meiss to buy my Christmas present, though whether they were heading for Woolworth's or Mappin and Webb I could not make Klara tell me. Where shopping is concerned Aunt Lucy tends to go to extremes. I dread the day when she discovers the British Home Stores.

I was terribly nervous about breaking Uncle Hugo's return to her, afraid that her transports of joy might bring on a heart attack, so I led up to it carefully by telling her that Pansy had been here. When I timidly added, 'Uncle Hugo's home,' she sat up and exclaimed, '*What?*' in tones of absolutely unmixed indignation and when I revealed how long he had been back, she went off into a perfect fusillade of furious monosyllables: 'Well! I . . . don't . . . know! Well! I mean!' I said that it was good that he was safe. 'Safe!' she said with indescribable scorn, and kept on peppering me with such exclamations for some time. I could not help glancing at little Hugo in his ringlets in the silver frame which Mrs Lockett is forced to polish every day, and at the pile of jungle books that littered the table with their dust-covers of ghastly masks, assegais and snakes. I might have reminded her of how she wept at the last words of one of them: 'They went down the track and were *swallowed up* in the jungle.' But all she was thinking of at that moment was the shower of barbed and poisoned postcards which she will soon sit down to compose.

This is not the first evidence we have had this week of the depravity of men. Fishtoft has been rumbled. He had been making extraordinary headway lately in gaining Aunt Lucy's affection, or at least tolerance; I don't think she could ever like a man who disagreed with her so often and (before he learned better) spoke slightingly of The Poets. But she had got to the point where she referred to him as a rough diamond (rough brickbat more likely Mrs Lockett remarked when she first heard this description). He had taken to turning up quite unannounced and once even brought a little bunch of chrysanthemums which Mrs Lockett put into a very large vase in order to display their small number and ragged condition. Sometimes he rang up and Aunt Lucy would have one of her fragmentary conversations, full of long pauses and unfinished sentences, murmured monosyllables and charming little giggles. I could not help admiring Fishtoft's stamina, standing gnawing his knuckles in some draughty phone box, playing a role for which he is so painfully miscast. Lately he had begun to exploit his own rudeness with great success. He would answer with a blunt No to questions which clearly called for the opposite, or abruptly invite himself to dinner adding roughly 'Why not?', if there were any hesitation in accepting him. To all this Aunt Lucy showed a sort of mock disapproval, shaking her head over his being so 'dreadful', but she did not dismiss him. I couldn't make it out. He was certainly getting money from her; perhaps it was more than we ever thought, and she felt as one does towards an expensive dress – having spent so much, one simply must wear it. Well, we shall never know, now. Wednesday was the Last Supper, and Klara Meiss the Judas. Fishtoft turned up unannounced, just in time for the grub, as he puts it, and after dinner Klara arrived looking flushed and excited as though she had had one yoghourt too many. She seemed put out at seeing Fishtoft and spent an hour trying unsuccessfully to outstay him, and at last said abruptly that she wanted to speak to Mrs Bender alone. Fishtoft, like an established favourite, said, 'Go on, don't mind me,' and this Aunt Lucy endorsed. Whereupon Klara Meiss drew from her capacious handbag a copy of 'The Crapyard, poems by Cedric Fishtoft' and some pages torn from *Woman's Own* and the *Knitting Weekly*, containing poems which the luckless Fishtoft had read out 'in this very room' as Aunt Lucy afterwards dramatically put it, passing them off as his own. *The Crapyard* did not at first have its full effect, as Aunt Lucy did not understand what it meant and she only reproached Fishtoft for having had something actually published without telling her. As Klara and I both declined her invitation to read from it, Fishtoft heroically stood up and declaimed his own death sentence, pausing in the middle to exclaim enthusiastically 'This is bloody good!' an opinion not shared by Aunt Lucy. *She* only murmured, 'Dear, how unpleasant,' and asked if they were all like that. Klara, stoking the fires of indignation, now proffered the torn-out pages, on which in frames of leaves or roses were some short poems, two of which I recognised at once. Aunt

Lucy was at first puzzled, prepared to congratulate him on having his poems published in such unexceptionable places, but the truth was soon explained to her and Fishtoft left, under a cloud. We do not know if he will ever come back.

As is the fate of servants who undeceive their masters, Klara Meiss has not got the recognition she deserves. Aunt Lucy has grown rather cool towards her; and keeps the poems amongst the vast disorder of sentimental souvenirs in her desk, as though they had indeed been written by one of her protégés.

Poor Aunt Lucy, it has been a week of shocks. Harvey, however, has provided a pleasant one. As this beastly security business seems to be taking so long, we decided it would be too complicated to go on pretending he was not here, and he has been several times to Bede Street although he declines to stay there, much to Aunt Lucy's amazement. She cannot understand why we should prefer Brown's Hotel and playfully accuses Harvey of taking me away from her. Her main anxiety is that I shall not be here for Christmas; there will be nobody but herself and Major Markette, she says, *crouching over the turkey*. She seems to have forgotten Roylance Cowlinshaw and that the wretched Fishtoft has also been invited – not to mention the fact that among the furious messages sent to Uncle Hugo there is sure to be the annual one reminding him that this was in all probability the last Christmas they would see, and they ought to spend it together. In fact, as Mrs Lockett has decreed a maximum of six, and as Harvey may very well still be here, it is beginning to look like Musical Chairs, or, as these things are seen here in life and death terms, Russian Sledges. Poor Fishtoft, I am afraid he has the greatest chance of ending up in the snow, though from the nutritional point of view his loss would be the greatest. I never saw anyone who ate with so much the air of stoking the boiler with anything combustible that came to hand.

Dear Christiane, it was lovely to hear from you and to know that you have not been pining unrequited for Harvey. It is so sensible of you not to fall in love with people. Without being in any way critical of Melville, I do wish you were married to somebody really nice and that you were as happy as I. I was hoping to see you soon as I was determined to come back to New York with Harvey; I am sure I could persuade him that our experimental separation is over. The security people, however, are *still* at it. Would you believe anybody could be so dilatory? If I were not persona non grata with Peter Bath I would suggest to him that he puts a psychologist on his staff: I mean you only have to *look* at Harvey! He, however, only says that things must take their course. If he is posted to some banana state, I suppose I shall have to consider it all my fault.

Harvey sends his best love. And so do I.

Cornelia

Mrs Bender to Sir Hugo Lamb Bede Street.
November 28th

My dear Hugo,

I have long suspected my neighbour Mr Viot of tampering with the mails, and I am absolutely certain that he abstracted or destroyed the letter you wrote telling me you were safely back home and that my dreadful anxieties about you were at an end. Mr Viot denies it in the most obstinate way and of course it must have happened several weeks ago, so it is difficult to prove, but I am persevering, with the help of the Post Office. What a brute you must have thought me when you got no answer! I hope you will forgive me, now that you know the explanation. I only heard of your return in the most roundabout way, by pure chance. Otherwise I might still be suffering, worrying and praying for you as I have been for the past months. Harvey explained to me that your letters from Zambia might very well not get through, so I suppose I should not grumble at not hearing from you then, though I wish I could have read them, fascinating as I am certain they were. It is really the worst of luck to be deprived of them here too! However, Mrs Lockett is going downstairs the moment the post arrives, in future, so the letters you write to me from now on will be safe. I am consulting Mr Cortis at once about how to set the law on Mr Viot, and hope he will soon get what he deserves.

I will not write a long letter – I want to hurry this one off so that you will understand the reason for my apparent heartlessness in not replying to you. I hope that your coming back in time for Christmas means that you will spend it with me here. If only we could relive those family Christmases when dear Father was alive! Now that there are only the two of us, we must try to do our best, for who knows, there may not be many more days of festivity left to us.

It has been delightful having Cornelia with me, but of course now that Harvey has returned she has rushed off and I am alone again, but I hope *you* will soon remedy that! I am sure you need rest and care after your strenuous travels in that savage country, and perhaps I may persuade you to a *long* visit this time.

Your loving sister, Lucia

Mrs Nieman to Mrs Lamb New York.
November 28th

Dear Cornelia,

Melville is back, he is rich, we are coming to London for

Christmas. He was left 75,000 dollars by a man he has not seen for years but now thinks may have been his father. Looking at his mother it is difficult to imagine, she is so tight-laced, but of course that was 34 years ago. This man was once the best friend of the family, then went off as people do here and got very rich without anybody knowing. Day before yesterday Melville walked into the apartment with this news. He seems well and has lost some weight, which is good. I asked what happened to Earl and he said he is okay. Then he asks me to choose a place to have a Christmas vacation. He said he would not have the nerve to come back, except for the money. He says he knew I would like that. It is true, but I think Earl Custance would like it also. On this subject Mel says nothing at all, except that he gave him some pretty things. Yesterday we went to Bonwits and bought some clothes. I let Mel choose them as his taste is better than mine – a silk dress, a coat and a beautiful fur. He wanted to buy more but I do not want to fritter the money.

Adam and Tigran came last night, they have one English girl between them, very nice and very good class. Prudence appears, décolletée, says she has just popped up and is very surprised to see Tigran. It is eerie how she knows when he is here. She has false eyelashes now, which gives her confidence but nothing else. Mel is very good and is not rude to her but afterwards he asks me to stop her coming because he can't stand the way she pronounces my name. I do not know why but I think this rather nice. I do not want to be unkind to her but I wish she would find a nice husband far away from here.

I am glad to know your Uncle Hugo is home. Harvey was worried though he did not show it. It is very nice to think we shall see you both so soon. We leave on the 20th.

Tigran says he gives me something to bring you. He is well and sends his love, Melville also. We shall be staying at the Hilton, I will telephone you as soon as we arrive. It will be nice to be in London with money, unlike every other time I was there.

Please give my love to Harvey.

Yours, Christiane

Postcard from Mrs Bender to Sir Hugo Lamb November 29th

I have spoken to Dr Dench about you and he says that you should take a *long* rest – that such a voyage at your age may well have delayed effects and you may suffer permanent damage if you do not take care. I have asked him to send you his prescription for the tonic he makes up for me when I have been overdoing things, and he is including a little note explaining the importance of taking exactly the correct amount. Soyez sage et prenez garde, Hugo, as dear Mother used to say!

Yours, Lucia

Mrs Lamb to Mrs Nash Brown's Hotel.
November 30th

Darling Mary,

I was so pleased to have your news. Hurrah for Larry! I am looking forward enormously to seeing you both and if only he has sculpted something under five feet high I will buy it and make everybody I know do the same. If you will let me know exactly when you are coming I will try to find you somewhere to stay. It will probably be a hotel, which I suppose Larry will find impossibly trite. I wish we were still at Edwardes Square, we could have crammed you all in somehow.

I ought to have answered your letter ages ago, if only to set your mind at rest about Uncle Hugo, who has been placidly sitting in Pigpound Lane for the past three weeks, but omitted to let us know it. The problem of Harvey and me has also been settled; here we are in Brown's Hotel and the lady in Maine is left lamenting. I do not mean to sound unsympathetic; I feel quite guilty at taking Harvey away from her when she has had him for such a short time. I promise I did not put any pressure on him. I suppose it was just the classic case of my being here and she there – though Harvey is not the sort of man to let a few thousand miles stand in his way. Oddly enough he has not made me promise to be good, or anything like that. Not one word has been said about *new leaves*. I am so grateful to him for this that I am determined in fact never to be unfaithful to him again.

This gratifying state of affairs is somewhat marred by the fact that repercussions from the brou-ha-ha have still not died down. No sooner have I got Tigran out of his predicament than my poor Harvey is in trouble. It is the Security Services again, and I am really getting very impatient with them. Tigran turns out to have an insecure brother and this seems to make them suspicious of Harvey, of all people. It is perfectly absurd, especially since Peter Bath was at Oxford with Harvey and must know that he is completely reliable. One would think he would want to make up for all the delay he caused over Tigran, but there is no moving these people. Poor Harvey is being very patient, but he is beginning to look a bit worn, and I am getting crosser about it every day. Pansy Sapling is in town and as she is such an ingenious child I am thinking of asking her advice. Do you think Minoprio would take on another injustice? Unfortunately his weapons seem to be headlines, and Harvey would not like that. I shall have to keep him as a last resort.

Christiane Nieman will be in London at the same time as you, isn't that fun? Her husband has just come back to her quite unexpectedly and without the slightest effort on her part. He has come into money and they are having a jaunt to celebrate their reunion. So you see we are all happily trooping back into Square One, a thing I never would have thought I could approve of so heartily. Aunt Lucy, of course, has never left it. Except for a certain ferment among the poets laureate, the great battle of her life goes on as usual, no quarter given or asked. The enemy does not change, and often has to be taken on three at a time, in the manner of Douglas Fairbanks. Christmas is providing us with plenty of Falstaffian skirmishes on the side. In spite of the fact that I am not actually staying in Bede Street, I haven't been shirking. Last week I went with her to Woolworth's as well as to Fortnums, and I do feel that anything reprehensible I have ever done has been paid for. Like Mr Woodhouse, Aunt Lucy goes very little into the world and is often astonished at what she hears. I did try to explain to her that Woolworth's was not like Marshall and Snelgrove, but nevertheless it came to her as a surprise. She wanted to know what the smell was, turning her nose round slowly with a sort of interested disgust. She wanted to know if the food was real; I suppose she thought it was Two Bad Mice food painted and glued to the plates. There was nowhere to sit down and command, so she entered into the spirit of the thing and toured the counters exclaiming '*Look* at that, isn't it *revolting*?' and commenting delightedly on 'their' abominable taste. She seemed to forget she was there to buy Christmas presents and ended up only with some small packets of soap which she could have got at Boots. She asked to see the manager, to complain at the absence of chairs, and to suggest that he sprayed the air with 'something fresher'. He was rather a young man and not so used to Aunt Lucys as some, and ended the interview so abruptly that she was convinced he had only gone away to fetch her a chair. She waited some time, leaning majestically on the green umbrella, sent two girls after him and then left, asking me reproachfully why I had brought her here. From there we went straight to Fortnums, where the high prices and the preponderance of Italian jerseys erased one astonishment with another. 'Are there no British goods?' she asked ringingly; and ended by buying two almost identical cream-coloured sweaters for herself and the smallest tin of pâté I have ever seen, for Roylance Cowlinshaw.

Aunt Lucy is very much looking forward to seeing you both, and to Larry's exhibition. I don't know whether to describe to her some of his works or let it burst on her quite unprepared. Incidentally, when we all meet, you won't forget my fictitious visits to you in the summer? It seems so long ago since the brou-ha-ha that you may have forgotten your part in it; but I should hate to have to try to explain it all to Aunt Lucy at this juncture.

I am planning to give a vast party at Bede Street, you and Christiane both being in London at the same time seems to be an excellent excuse, and there are several things to be celebrated. Then there are all the nice people who had me to dinner while I was alone. A party, in fact, seems imperative, so don't get yourselves booked up for every night of the week, while you are here.

Harvey has just come in, and sends his love.

Yours, Cornelia

Postcard from Mrs Bender to Sir Hugo Lamb

November 31st

I found this picture of the dear old house and thought you would like to have it.

Mrs Lockett has insisted on getting your room ready, and you may therefore descend on us at any time. Her devotion is really quite touching and she is looking forward so much to your visit.

Lucia

Message to Postman

Please handle this card carefully as it is *unique*.

Mrs Lamb to Tigran Leontyev

Brown's Hotel.
December 3rd

Darling Tigran,

I wonder whether you have been able to contact your brother? I do hope so. Perhaps you could persuade him to come to America and mend his ways? I wish you could; it might save poor Harvey's career if you could do it quick enough. We have heard nothing more, he is still in suspense and I am just wondering whether I should try to give things a tiny push. As it happens I have just had a fascinating conversation with Pansy Sapling which may turn out to be useful in this direction. She has been in London for the past week or so, staying at the Strand Palace Hotel, looking up her old friends in Fleet Street and bombarding the Prime Minister with awkward questions about animal exploitation. When he kindly explained to her that Home Secretaries make the laws, she transferred her attention to the unfortunate Peter Bath; and having been turned away from his office by misguided secretaries, she resourcefully went to his home where she stumbled upon what she considers to be a major scandal. At any rate, within five minutes it had become her prime consideration, quite superseding the larger issues of the law. It appears that there turned up at Peter Bath's house several years ago, a large dog whose ownership could not be traced, and so it was adopted and lived, like an Edwardian child, chiefly with the servants, but making guest appearances in the drawing-room. Like many beauties it turned out to have some irritating habits; so that when it decorated the parquet like a beautiful rug or ran gracefully about the lawn, Peter and Diana would be congratulated on a valuable possession; but on the other hand it was 'Cook's dog has been running the sheep again' or 'Cook's dog has buried the leg of lamb'. After several years of this schizophrenic existence, a crisis occurred when the cook was pensioned off and proposed to take the dog with her. Diana Bath would not hear of it and a battle began which should have ended when Peter Bath resourcefully found a flat for the old lady's retirement in a block close to the town, where dogs were not allowed. Mrs Cavendish (the cook) riposted by persuading the owners of the block that a large dog would be just the thing to combat vandalism. Her case was bolstered by a providential burglary, and that round went to her. At this point, however, Diana Bath, who is a managing woman, took the dog up to London where it has been ever since. All this Pansy Sapling in her disguise as a harmless little girl got out of the Bath's London housekeeper, over a cup of cocoa. Feeling in the village, the housekeeper said, is running high. There were rumours that the dog had been shot, to end the argument. Mrs Cavendish had been to the police. Peter Bath had tried her with two expensive puppies, both of which she rejected, thus further burdening his household, as he could not get them off his hands. Pansy is very indignant. She says Knightsbridge is no place for a large dog, and she has become a fierce partisan of the cook, on democratic grounds. She is very anxious to right this wrong, but I see it as a stick to beat the beastly Bath with. I am sure we can use it somehow, but it must be done with incredible circumspection. Pansy is coming to tea tomorrow to discuss plans. I have not said much to her about Harvey's security troubles, because I did promise to keep it as secret as possible, but I had to give her just a hint of it, to prevent her doing anything drastic before the best advantage could be got out of her discoveries. After all, perhaps if I could soothe the angry cook and restore the dog to Peter, he might clear Harvey out of sheer gratitude. I suppose it is unlikely, but just the same it would surely do no harm to put him in a benevolent mood.

I must say it is all rather unsettling. Pansy Sapling when crusading is so like an explosive which may be set off by the slightest jar and blow up entirely the wrong objective. Do you remember how splendid she was at Pott Shrigley shooing off the reporters while we sat in the attic eating apples? She sends her regards to you, by the way.

Isn't it good news that Melville has come back and that he has inherited all that money? It will be so nice for Christiane to have something to be prudent with. I am looking forward very much to seeing them in London, but I wish you could come with them! Melville could easily pay your fare. If I thought there was the slightest hope I would write to Christiane about it, but I know it would be no use. I can't make her do things, it is always the other way about. She would say you are a terrible spendthrift, and ought not to be encouraged.

Au revoir, dear Tigran, I shall write again soon.

Your, Cornelia

Mrs Lamb to Mrs Nieman Brown's Hotel. December 3rd

Darling Christiane,

I always knew you deserved something very nice to happen to you and it is most satisfactory to know that for once a legacy has fallen into the right hands. We will have a marvellous party to celebrate – oddly enough Mary and Larry Nash are coming to London too – he is going to exhibit his works in some long-suffering gallery in Cork Street. He has only once, so far as I know, shown anything of his to the public; then, somebody called him 'The Maillot of the scrap metal yard', which seems discouraging, but that was in the provinces and besides the critic is dead. I had a slightly rattled letter from Mary, who has the task of bringing Larry, the four children and a lorry load of unintelligible works of art to London and being responsible for their well-being while they are here. But she sounded quite cheerful and will be more so when she knows that Uncle Hugo and Harvey are both back in their appointed places. I am sure she would like to be able to fit Nan comfortably into the pattern too, but I suppose one can't have everything. It is a pity she doesn't know how chastened I feel, it would give her great satisfaction, but I can't quite bring myself to confess it, perhaps because she has been telling me off one way and another, all her life.

I do hope that by the time I see you all our troubles will really be over. Everything is by no means rosy yet, as I told you, and in fact since my last letter things have become slightly more complicated. We have heard nothing; Peter Bath is completely mum, and of course Harvey won't ask, and I thought I saw a way to hurry things up a little bit, using Pansy Sapling, who seemed to have been sent by a merciful providence to help me do so. Unfortunately, her large acquaintance among politicians and newspapermen seems to have gone to her head. She has become much too big for her boots – not literally, as she has begun a single-minded effort to stunt her growth with cigarettes, so as to preserve the childish stature which is such an asset in the peculiar career she has embarked upon. She is becoming daily more adept at the role of the pretty little girl, somewhat soft in the head, who has somehow wandered into the Vatican and naturally ends up by giving orders to the Pope. Her success at this sort of thing is making her quite uncontrollable and it is maddening to see all this power running to waste. I did want to use just a little of it to jerk Peter Bath out of his inertia, but I feel now that it is somewhat too nuclear for the purpose, and that somebody – I hope it is not Harvey – may get blown to bits. H., of course, knows nothing whatever about all this, and neither does anyone else except Tigran, who is the only person I can explain it all to without the risk of a telling off. *You* would give me one, I am sure, dear Christiane, so I will say no more about it.

Things are fairly quiet at Bede Street, though every day Aunt Lucy repeats that Christmas is on us, as though it were the fatal stone in Aïda. Fishtoft has really had his congé, as Aunt L. herself puts it, though not without a little struggle on both sides. Aunt Lucy clandestinely bought a copy of *The Crapyard* and since she could not expose me or Klara Meiss to such a thing, pored over it herself with the aid of a dictionary until she was completely convinced of its infamy. As for him, he came round last week 'on the sponge' as Mrs Lockett calls it, but though dinner was on the table he was kept out of the dining-room, headed off from the drinks cupboard and finally routed without even the opportunity of pocketing a few snuff-boxes. Since then he has telephoned once or twice but clearly hope is fading. He is definitively overboard, and Aunt Lucy has sailed away like a ship leaving a sinking rat. The sequel to his dismissal is the reappearance of Spencer, as though by the working of some natural law. I went round to Bede Street unexpectedly last night and found them snuggled up by the fire, and with no sign of the wretched Linda. Spencer looked like a smug nestling who has successfully ousted the cuckoo, and well he might. He is safe from poor Fishtoft's dilemma – he is very capable of writing his own rubbish. Aunt Lucy beckoned me in with finger to lip and told Spencer to go on reading, and I came in for one of his longer poems which Mrs Lockett and I call Gray's Allergy. It has a large number of stanzas and a somnolent rhythm which enables Aunt Lucy to have a little doze and at the end of it we were all rewarded with a small glass of Madeira.

So you see all around us the status quo is reasserting itself like some frightful force of nature. *You* have always liked the status quo, haven't you, Christiane? But you must admit that it is a good thing for it to be rattled about a bit.

Harvey has just come into the room and says how very glad he is to know of Melville's return; the money, he says rather sternly, is a secondary benefit. He also says he always knew that Melville would not stay away long because despite appearances he is a sensible man. I hope Melville will take this as a compliment. We both look forward immensely to seeing you. Telephone me as soon as you arrive.

Yours, Cornelia

Postcard from Mrs Bender to Sir Hugo Lamb

The fiend has struck again! *Again* your letter has been seized – it is a week since my postcard to you and I know you must have written. Would you please write to me registered this time – he can surely not snatch it from the postman. In any case I shall warn the Post Office. Reply to this by return and then I shall know when to expect your letter, and Mrs Lockett will be lurking on the stairs. Perhaps we shall catch him red-handed!

Your Lucia

Mrs Lamb to Tigran Leontyev

Brown's Hotel.
December 7th

Darling Tigran

Since I last wrote to you things have deteriorated slightly and though I would not confess this to anybody in the world but you, I am beginning to feel a little nervous. Of course I should not have mentioned to Pansy Sapling my plans for galvanising Peter Bath; I might have known she would translate them into action without the delay of actually thinking them out. It is a question of too much and too soon: she has fired all her guns and seems to be enjoying the resultant racket. After all, as I need to remind myself from time to time, she is only eleven.

Instead of coming to tea with me to discuss our strategy, the wretched child went straight to the Home Office and, slipping through the outer defences, was finally netted in an inner office where she came up against several secretaries, notably one E. Rawsthorne, who was unwise enough to smile at her and address her as 'little girl'. It made her very indignant, and I sympathise as I once had a telephone conversation with this Rawsthorne and he took a very similar tone. When she could not convince them that it would be in the personal interest of the Home Secretary to see her, she went away and composed an anonymous letter in which she threatened Peter Bath with a trouncing from the *Daily Mirror* if he did not allow the dog to go back to the country where it belonged. She kindly included Harvey's security clearance in her demands, and probably an amnesty for all guinea-pigs as well – I was not really attending to the final phrases of the letter, which she proudly read to me over the telephone; I was hoping so very much, though I knew it was groundless, that she had not actually sent it. Now we are left to wonder what will happen next. I don't know how far a letter like that would get – whether P. Bath would actually see it, and there is nobody to ask but Harvey. The unfortunate Peter Bath has two days in which to comply with the demands. Tomorrow I am going to take Pansy out to lunch and try to get a stay of execution. I would very much like to persuade her to go back to Cheshire, but I am afraid it is never easy to get the genie back into the bottle.

I do hope everything is going well for you, darling Tigran. In Christiane's last letter she mentioned you twice and actually sent me your love, I suppose she is mellowed by her good fortune. She also said she was bringing me something from you – I am looking forward to *that* immensely. Meantime, I send you my love.

Your Cornelia

Postcard from Sir Hugo Lamb to Mrs Bender December 8th

I have not written and since you know I am back I see no necessity to do so. I am perfectly well, so long as I stay here where I am comfortable. London is no rest to me as you know and in any case I am far too busy for visiting.

Kindly send me no more postcards.

Hugo

Tigran Leontyev to Mrs Lamb New York. December 11th

Darling Princess,

I wrote my brother in East Berlin and invited him over to my place for Christmas. He is very serious man but I don't think he is spying. Janek saw him a while ago and said he was working on computers and very prosperous. I have not seen him in fifteen years and hope he doesn't get a wife in the meantime or there will be rather crowd in my apartment.

I hope you like the little thing Christiane brings you, I hope it reminds you of me. Come soon to United States where I welcome you with open arms. I hope your troubles are soon over and you have a lovely Christmas, darling. Be happy.

Love and kisses, Tigran

From the Daily Mirror, *December 12th*

Home Secretary in Village Squabble

The Home Secretary, whose speech on law and order in the House of Commons on Tuesday caused a row, is having a spot of bother with law and order on his own doorstep. The sleepy little village of Green End is divided, and conversation at the Cross Keys has only one subject these days. And it is not rising prices, or the weather.

Bone of contention

The bone of contention is a dog called Rusty. Some people say he rightfully belongs to Mrs Cavendish, who at the ripe age of 76 has just moved into Sunset House, near High Wycombe, after twelve years as cook to Mr and Mrs Bath at the High Hall, Green End. 'Rusty was with me all those years,' said Mrs Cavendish today, 'and now that I am in the evening of my life I want him here, but he has been taken away and I cannot discover his whereabouts.'

Gracious Mansion

When I went to see Mrs Diana Bath (43) at the Home Secretary's gracious eight-bedroomed mansion on the edge of the village, she told me that she was very fond of the dog and had always considered it as one of the family. She made no secret of the fact that the dog was in London, but added that she often left him there as company for her teenage daughter. 'There is really no problem at all,' she said and laughingly added, 'it is all a storm in a teacup.'

I wonder.

Postcard from Mrs Bender to
Sir Hugo Lamb December 12th

Harvey and Cornelia are bitterly disappointed – they had so hoped to see you before they go back to America again, perhaps for years. It is unlike you to ignore *them* – I do beg you, for your own sake, to see your doctor. Dr Dench says it may be something physical, and quite simple to cure, if only you will take advice about it now, we shall have our dear old Hugo back again! Soyez sage, Hugo – if only dear Mother were here to direct you!

Your loving sister, Lucia

Postcard from Sir Hugo Lamb to
Mrs Bender December 14th

I have instructed the Post Office to deliver *no more postcards whatsoever.*

H. L.

Mrs Lamb to Tigran Leontyev Brown's Hotel.
December 16th

Darling Tigran,

You are an angel to ask your brother over but will he get a visa? If he does, that will surely prove that he is all right and *that* ought to satisfy these insatiable security people. But will he want to come? I suppose he can spy in America as well as anywhere else, though I hope he does not, for your sake. Do let me know what happens; things are rather uncomfortable here and anything in the way of good news would be a welcome novelty.

Yesterday Harvey came in from a visit to the Home Office and found me in the lounge with a nice old bird from Maine, and without even letting me introduce him to her, whisked me into the lift and in stony silence to our room where he shut the door and took out of his pocket a copy of Pansy's anonymous letter. It was stamped SECRET all over, but I recognised the spelling at once. He gave it to me and asked in the most awful voice whether I knew anything about it. Darling Tigran what a frightful moment! I simply had to lie, for all our sakes. Then he said, I suppose that child wrote it. My head became a perfect jumble of everybody I had ever met who could possibly be blamed – the most unlikely people, like Uncle Hugo, Margot, even Major Markette. In the end I had to come back to poor Pansy. (After all, she is the only one of us too young to go to prison.) Luckily, her ransom note was so vaguely worded that I was able to convince Harvey that she knew nothing about his security troubles but must have been taking up the cudgels on his behalf, in her childish way, because of something I said to her about his leaving his job in New York after such a short time. It sounded pretty lame, I must admit, but I impressed on Harvey that she was an eccentric child with a tender heart who would champion any cause and moreover life in London was giving her folie de grandeur and making her do all sorts of peculiar things. Harvey said he supposed it was she who had instigated the attack, as he put it, on Peter Bath in the *Daily Mirror* (cutting enclosed). It was no good disagreeing, so he went off and telephoned Colonel Sapling to come at once, though what good that poor old gentleman will be I really don't know. Of course they want to see Pansy but luckily they don't know where she is at the moment and I am hoping they don't find her before this afternoon, when we have arranged to meet. I hope I can persuade her to keep quiet about my part in the affair, though it doesn't seem quite fair since I couldn't do the same for her. I suppose she will be bundled off to Pott Shrigley, which might be just as well. After all, she has shot her bolt, and can do no more for the cause, unless she can find another Cabinet Minister with a guilty secret. Her efforts in this case seem to have been largely wasted, which may discourage her. So far as the art of blackmail is concerned, she seems to have a good deal to learn.

I hope after this afternoon to have no more to do with this business, it is getting rather exhausting, and threatens to throw a blight over Christmas, which at Bede Street is already being anticipated like a well-documented cyclone. Aunt Lucy frightened us all by a temporary enthusiasm for one of those indignant letters in *The Times*, which contrast the groaning boards of Christmas with the bowls of rice in other parts of the world, and suggested we should forgo all alcohol and choose a smaller pudding. Luckily, her indignation has been deflected towards the Insurance Company, who have just written to say that as she has only lost *one* of her diamond earrings, they cannot pay for both. She is sending the other to them by registered post, hoping to shame them into payment.

Well, Tigran, I must end this and go to my assignation with Pansy. We have arranged to meet at the zoo, and will probably end up in the Director's office. I don't know whether that will do any good, but you never know – any ally would be welcome just now. I hope she is not in her most militant mood, and will not be inspired to return after nightfall, with her skeleton keys.

I will write to you again soon and in the meantime send you all my love.

Cornelia

From the Buckinghamshire Gazette, *December 17th*

Where is Mr Bath's Dog?

Accusations are being made here that the Home Secretary, the Rt. Hon. Peter Bath, M.P., has had his dog destroyed rather than allow it to go to the woman who some say was its rightful owner, Mrs Elizabeth Cavendish of Sunset House, High Wycombe. The dispute arose when Mrs Cavendish left the employ of Mr Bath, with whom she was cook for a number of years. She had always thought of the dog as her own and wished to take it with her, but was not allowed to do so. Mr Bath was not available for comment, but Mrs Bath told us that the dog was alive and well and was being kept for the time being in London, as he had to visit the chiropodist.

'If the dog is alive, let us see him,' said Mr Tasman Gates, the Youth Leader, who is organising a petition here on Mrs Cavendish's behalf. He went on to state that Mr Bath's action was high-handed in the extreme and typical of the arrogant attitudes of the present Government. Few here would agree with him. Mr Bath is a respected member of the community. It is felt, however, that a generous gesture on his part would heal the breach in this otherwise closely knit community.

From the Daily Express, *December 18th*

There is no peace for poor Mr Bath these days. As soon as he leaves the turmoil of the parliamentary scene for a quiet week-end in the country he is plunged into controversy which closely concerns his own family. It is all about the ownership of a dog and is being taken very seriously by the inhabitants of the village of Green End. There is even some talk of the dog being destroyed but let us hope that the Home Secretary will in this case exercise his prerogative of reprieve.

From the News of the World, *December 18th*

It may seem a small thing in this age of catastrophes, that an old-age pensioner in a remote country village is pining away, this Christmas, for the companionship of a dog. But to Mrs Cavendish, an 80-year-old widow, it is not a small thing. Her happiness depended on Rusty, a golden retriever, with whom she had hoped to share the loneliness of her retirement. And who has deprived her of this comfort in her old age? Our own Home Secretary, the Rt. Hon Peter Bath, M.P., the man to whom we entrust justice and from whom we expect mercy, especially at this time of the year.

Mr Bath's claim to this valuable pet may well be justified. But whatever the rights and wrongs of the case it is surely incumbent upon him in this season of goodwill to make a generous gesture, to waive his rights in favour of one who is so much less fortunate than himself. No one will think the worse of him for doing so, and one old lady will be made very happy.

A small thing? We do not think so.

From The Times, *December 20th*

The vulnerability of those in public life is strikingly illustrated by the attention which is being focused upon a trivial incident in the household of Mr Peter Bath, an incident which would pass completely unnoticed were it not for the position which Mr Bath holds in the Government. Unfortunately a section of the press hostile to the present administration has inflated the matter out of all proportion, and we are now faced with absurd situation in which one of our ablest ministers may be forced to resign over a matter which is of no conceivable interest except to the two or three people concerned. At a time of economic crisis and when clouds are again gathering in the Middle East, it is surely time that we learned to ignore the calls upon our indignation made perhaps in good faith, but exploited for unworthy motives.

From the Daily Mail, *December 20th*

Cabinet Split over the resignation of
Home Secretary
Archbishop calls for Common Sense
Threat of Strike by Prison Warders

Prison Warders throughout the country have threatened to go on strike if Mr Peter Bath resigns his position as Home Secretary. This is the latest and most serious development in the row which has been caused by accusations against the Home Secretary of misappropriating a valuable dog at his home in Buckinghamshire. Mrs Elizabeth Cavendish, who is bringing a suit against Mr Bath, has fallen ill and was not available today but friends said she was resolved to fight to the end. The Cabinet, which is divided on the issue of Mr Bath's possible resignation, is to be called to a special meeting at Chequers tomorrow. The Prime Minister, a lifelong member of the Tailwaggers' Club, is clearly in a very difficult position, but a statement is expected from him tomorrow evening.

The Archbishop of Canterbury said on television last night that if the parties to the dispute could come together in an atmosphere of quiet and calm, away from the glare of publicity, and discuss their differences peaceably, he was sure common sense would prevail.

Mrs Lamb to Tigran Leontyev Brown's Hotel.
December 28th

Darling Tigran,

The bracelet you sent me is absolutely adorable – if only, if *only* I could thank you in person! Christiane typically refused to let me have it until Christmas Day. I put it on then and have worn it ever since. At first I could not think how you could have found anything I like so much; then I realised that I would probably feel like that about anything you gave me. Thank you, darling. It will indeed remind me of you some day, perhaps in a decade or two, when I might need reminding.

Christmas was fairly enjoyable, considering the circumstances. Poor Harvey's security clearance didn't come through but worse than that the business of P. Bath and his dog has become a sort of cause célèbre; Pansy's little leak to the *Daily Mirror* became a perfect flood and in no time Peter Bath had offered to resign, the Cabinet split, Archbishops and Trade Unions got into the act and there was dark talk of the whole thing being a political manoeuvre to oust the wretched Bath. Thank goodness, in the past few days the furore has more or less disappeared from the papers. On the front pages at least its place has been taken by a statement from a doctor that turkey causes cancer of the stomach. Unattractive as this seasonal message is, it is at least a relief to be able to pick up a paper without dreading the headlines. The worst of it all is that it is doing poor Harvey no good at all. If Peter Bath still has any power he is not very likely now to exercise it on Harvey's behalf; and it is only a little comforting to know that if he does resign his place will be taken (so Murray Bassett assures me) by Robert Moxon, who is a nice man and a good friend of Harvey's. He is a man whose only real interest is in racing motor cars, but is said to have a brilliant political future. He started life in the College of Arms and is known to his friends as Triumph Herald Extraordinary.

Harvey himself is taking it all very philosophically. He was furious for about three days, and could not really find a suitable target, which made it worse. He had Pansy in for a formal dressing-down, but I am afraid it didn't do much good. She told me afterwards that he was smashing, and that if things did not go better for him she would see what she could do. He also lectured old Colonel Sapling about the responsibilities of the parent, and has been rather stern towards me; but he melted considerably during Christmas and now only sometimes looks at me sadly, as though still wondering whether I am to blame. He managed to be very jolly at Bede Street, where of course Aunt Lucy knows nothing about it all and constantly congratulated him on his nice long stay in England, away from the neurotic pressures of American society.

I think Christmas dinner could be counted a success in

spite of our state of suspense, and the ill-assorted guests – Major Markette, Roylance Cowlinshaw, Harvey and me, and Klara Meiss thrown in to balance the sexes. She kept up an astonishing standard of raillery throughout the meal while Roylance and the Major concentrated on getting enough to eat – easier than usual since Harvey had rather high-handedly taken over the carving and serving from Aunt Lucy and was handing out portions which made her flinch. The Major's eloquence at the moment is devoted to people who throw things at football matches. They should be stood out on the pitch and stoned by goalkeepers and referees. The toast of Absent Friends was very affecting; 'poor Hugo' came first, lost to us through mental incapacity, then 'poor Spencer' lost, for this evening at least, to the onerous necessities of married life, and the rest were lumped together in a murmur amongst raised glasses. Roylance, who was sitting next to me, whispered roguishly that he knew who I was thinking of. He sends you his kind regards, as usual.

Boxing Day is traditionally the occasion for serving up the funeral baked meats to Poor Maud, with small amounts of beetroot. It is also Mrs Lockett's evening off, and the most elaborate arrangements are made for Aunt Lucy to produce the entire meal herself. It is a peculiar ritual involving innumerable journeys out of the dining-room, dishes rattling to Aunt Lucy's quavering walk, which is noticeably feebler than on ordinary days. She spends a lot of time in the kitchen beforehand, exclaiming that cooking is rather fun, but it really is difficult for her to give up her role of overseer and take to manual labour and no food at all would be forthcoming if it were not for certain guests, chosen for this purpose – in this case Klara Meiss and me. Hot boiled potatoes are the high spot of this culinary adventure – Aunt Lucy excitedly hands forks to her helpers and begs them to see whether they are done, stands by while the dangerous steam escapes, and chooses the dish to put them in. We are all exhausted by the time we sit down and the level of the sherry decanter plummets alarmingly. I suspect Poor Maud of having a furtive nip from time to time, as well as myself. I thought I would dilute the proceedings this year so I boldly invited Christiane and Melville to come in afterwards for coffee. It is so nice to have Christiane in town! I haven't seen nearly as much of her as I would have liked. Harvey thought it was a bit hard to ask her to this particular occasion – Poor Maud is not everybody's choice – but Christiane is so bien-élevé, she positively enjoys behaving well in trying circumstances and I did want Melville to see Aunt Lucy's china. *He* went down very well. She told him that for an American he was very polite, and seemed amazed that he knew the difference between china and porcelain. I suppose they get used to it; he, at any rate, was quite impervious and in the mysterious way that people sometimes do, appeared to become instantly devoted to Aunt Lucy for no evident reason. Christiane listened with apparent fascination to Poor Maud's seasonal tales – the woman whose Spanish cook killed two guests with Horse-chestnut Stuffing, the turkey that had come from abroad with a bottle of brandy inside it and exploded on the table, piercing the butler with slivers of glass. It was altogether rather a successful evening. Now we are resting on our laurels and husbanding our resources for an enormous party which we are giving at Bede Street tomorrow. I persuaded Harvey to it, and he persuaded Aunt Lucy. She is of course in a state of excitement and alarm. In spite of the fact that Harvey is paying for it and I am doing all the organisation, there is a great deal of worrying to be done. She spent all this morning wandering about the flat wondering what 'they' will do to it, and reproaching me for not having started to cut some sandwiches. She is sure no food will be delivered; in spite of her absolute faith in Fortnums, she feels that a tragic fate will intervene. She was terrified by the amount of drink that has been ordered. Harvey has had to give Mrs Lockett instructions to monitor the telephone in case she tries to cancel or at least modify it. I am hoping that she will occupy herself for most of tomorrow in resting and dressing, and that sheer numbers will muffle any social crisis that may arise from the rather peculiar mixture of guests: I can't help speculating about the impact of Larry Nash on Major Markette, and I don't suppose the Home Secretary (if he is still in office by then) will be very pleased to see Pansy Sapling. I just sent invitations to everybody I wanted to see though I am not sure *why* I want to see some of them. Of course the only person I really want to see is you, but I shall have to make do with about sixty second-bests. Aunt Lucy entered thoroughly into the spirit of the thing and wrote off to various cronies she has not seen for years, and even to a retired Admiral she has never met, but felt sorry for after reading about his poverty in the paper. Mr. Mortleman is coming and his letter of acceptance sounded as though he had only been to three other parties in his life. Being a millionaire does tend to keep one unspoilt, in many ways.

I am sitting in the writing-room, which is dark, with shaded lamps, hoping to avoid being summoned back to Bede Street. I have just opened the curtains and it is snowing, hard enough to make the street quiet. The Americans have gone to the bar and there is only an old gentleman who has gone to sleep holding the *Illustrated London News*. This place reminds me of the Hôtel de Lys, though it is not in the least like it. I suppose all hotels remind me of the

Hôtel de Lys. Do you remember the cross-eyed boy who did your shoes?

Write to me some time, darling Tigran. A very very happy New Year, from

Your Cornelia

I had sealed this up but tore it open again to tell you that Harvey has just come in and *everything is all right*! His security clearance has come through and he is perfectly eligible to take the most responsible job in the world, without any danger of his passing state secrets to me, me passing them to you and you to your brother. It is such a relief that I don't quite know what to do – no more now, H. has gone to get champagne.

Yours, C.

Tigran Leontyev to Mrs Lamb

New York.
December 30th

Darling Cornelia,

Thank you a million for beautiful glass lion, it is in place of honour on my shelf and looks terrific. I wish you could see it. My brother did not show up, he went to Moscow for Christmas but I had a card from him, first in years. He sounds quite cheerful.

I only just recovered from Christmas so please excuse short letter. After New Year I work terribly hard, earn a lot of money and come and see you, so don't go away. I never forget our wonderful times darling.

Love and kisses, Tigran

Mrs Lamb to Mrs Nieman

Bede Street.
January 4th

Darling Christiane,

I do hope you had a good trip home. I wish you were

still here – I don't seem to have seen nearly enough of you while you were in London.

Far from ruining Harvey's career, our little brou-ha-ha seems to have improved it – he is going to Paris as Counsellor in March. He is very pleased about it and so am I, except that I was looking forward to being in the same town as you. You will have to persuade Melville to spin out his riches, or earn some more, so that you can come to Europe more often.

Wasn't it a good party? And wasn't it an astonishing piece of luck that Harvey's business was settled just in time to make it a real celebration! Its reverberations went on for some days after you left. Mr Mortleman telephoned me from Melbourne to ask for Roylance Cowlinshaw's address; he has commissioned him to paint an enormous portrait of his kitchen staff. Pansy Sapling is still in London raising support for some unholy scheme which she and Albert Minoprio are cooking up together; I am afraid they are in for it again at Downing Street. Yesterday Margot telephoned and said she had seen Peter Bath in Jules's Bar the day after the party with a most peculiar-looking woman, I am sure as the result of our aphrodisiac food. It is very pleasant to think that one's hospitality has results.

I do hope you will decide to come back to London before too long. Aunt Lucy would very much like to see you both again. She can't get over Melville being so sympathique and is convinced that he must have had an English governess. She is greatly relieved that Harvey is not staying in New York, and often congratulates him on taking her advice and looking for a more civilised place.

Mary and Larry have gone back to Suffolk quite pleased with the success of the exhibition. It received the classic accolade, on the last day but one, of an angry art lover attempting to break up something called Spheroid 23 with an axe. In spite of invoking the Venus de Milo as he did so, the axe bent; Larry was delighted with the resultant dents and lectured the assembled crowd on morphosis and the beauty of accidents. I don't think he sold very much but this incident at least increased the attendance on the last day, and got his name into the papers.

Harvey has gone away for a few days so I have come back to Bede Street after a piteous summons from Aunt Lucy who has retired to bed with a slight temperature caused, I believe, from accidentally seeing the bill from Fortnums for the party food. She is convinced that nobody realised how expensive, or even how good, it was, especially Uncle Hugo for whom if she had known he was coming, she would have had some cheese sandwiches made. She is in an amiable mood, however, as Spencer is naturally discovering the burdens of marriage and comes quite often to lay them down at her bedside. Klara Meiss is also in attendance most days, so I am as much at leisure as it is possible to be under Aunt Lucy's roof, and am finding this dilatory existence rather enjoyable, particularly as it is not for long; as soon as Harvey gets back there will be a lot to do preparatory to our move to Paris. You will be glad to know that I am waiting for him, before taking any decisions or making any arrangements that concern us both. I have somewhat recovered from the mood I was in, just before you left, when I felt I agreed with Mr Thurber that woman's place is in the wrong, but nevertheless I am determined not to commit any more bêtises; you have no idea how angelic he has been lately, and we are absolutely never to quarrel again. I shall go out into the street and bring in one of those road signs which say 'Give Way', and set it up where I can see it, as a reminder.

Love to Mel, and of course to Tigran if you see him.

Yours, Cornelia

PS.—I had a Christmas card from M. Bellavance with the clairvoyant hope of seeing me in Paris. But of course as a Counsellor's wife, there could be nothing like *that*!

Mrs Lamb to Tigran Leontyev Bede Street.

January 7th

Darling,

Harvey has gone to Paris, so here I am again in Bede Street, seeing Aunt Lucy through a rather enjoyable attack of flu which keeps her in bed but does not diminish her powers in any way. She sits against the pillows in a mob cap and a very beautiful bed-jacket, issuing written orders so as to spare her voice. In the evenings, in a different hat, she holds levées – strictly forbidden by Dr Dench, and concealed from him by a series of elaborate alibis. Uncle Hugo has of course been summoned but has said he is going instead to Lusaka. Undeterred, she is determined to spend her convalescence at Wood Cottage, and has sent him a catalogue of comfortable beds.

He turned up, incredibly enough, on the day of our party. Although his arrival was completely unexpected, Aunt Lucy dragged him into the drawing-room without even allowing him to let go of his ditty-bag, struck a glass for silence and announced 'My brother Hugo!' as though he had been the expected lion of the occasion. He would have gone away again at once if it had not been for the fact that the first person she introduced him to was Margot Bassett in lace pyjamas and three pairs of eyelashes. He adores pretty women and so was trapped; and shortly afterwards when confronted by Albert Minoprio some happy chance or perhaps a mysterious instinct caused him to launch into a furious attack on democracy, and so he stayed, drinking tumblers of milk and champing asparagus rolls and smoked salmon sandwiches without, as Aunt Lucy pointed out to him, the slightest idea of what was in them. (She very quickly forgot that she had not paid for the food and was scandalised by the inroads made on it by the ravening hordes, as she called our guests.) He dossed down for the night in the large spare room and left again the next day without, so far as we know, leaving any unfortunate mementoes behind. I don't think he had time to fix up any booby traps.

It was a very successful party and of course for Harvey and me it couldn't have been better timed, to celebrate the removal of the cloud we've been under for so long. Peter Bath's resignation, by the way, was not accepted by the Prime Minister, and the restoration of the dog to rural life more or less repaired his image in the village, and presumably in the world. Television cameras recorded the ceremonial handing over of the dog to Mrs Cavendish, a course which, according to Peter's statement, had been his intention all along, delayed only by the fact that the dog had been having treatment for ingrowing toenails. We are reliably informed that Mrs Cavendish has since secretly returned poor Rusty to the Bath household because he did not get on with the budgie which she was given by village subscription. The Baths already have the two large puppies which Peter unavailingly tried to present to Mrs Cavendish, which is a judgement on Diana, whose volte-face was caused solely by the fact that the dog ate two Bokhara rugs while it was in London. I was rather surprised that Peter Bath turned up at our party considering all the trouble we have caused him; and he was clearly even more surprised to be confronted by Pansy Sapling, who he must have supposed had been run out of good society. She was not in the least abashed, commended him for doing the right thing in the end, and immediately bearded him on the subject of blood sports; I hope he felt some sympathy for the victims as she hunted him remorselessly from room to room. At the end of the party he got rather drunk and lamented the hardships of a politician's life. He assured me very earnestly that nothing at all that had happened had had the slightest effect on Harvey's security clearance; it had all been a matter of the usual channels, avenues and stones, and he himself had never been in any doubt about the outcome; so I suppose Pansy might have spared her pains.

It was a peculiar assortment of guests, but everybody seemed to enjoy themselves. Mr Mortleman was in a happy mood; he had just returned from an international conference, where he had been able to introduce Mr Quick to Herr Schnell. He was his usual retiring self until near the end when after three glasses of champagne, which is far beyond his average, he tried to buy Admiral Drummer for his band. *This* gentleman, who had been invited by Aunt Lucy sight unseen, concentrated on eating as much as possible in the given time and was affable to everybody except Major Markette, in whom he instantly recognised an occupant of the same boat. Aunt Lucy introduced them to each other several times and seemed delighted with the similarity of their age and station; and they were both heard to refer to each other as 'idiotic old buffers' in different parts of the room. Larry Nash was in splendid form in corduroys and a ragged red neckerchief. He made a tremendous pass at Linda, who Spencer had brought despite strict orders from Aunt Lucy not to do so. He also unaccountably attached himself to an old acquaintance of Aunt Lucy's, a lady married to an impotent clergyman, who is alleged to have had a baby by artificial insemination. She was a neighbour of Aunt Lucy's in Gloucestershire, and the provider was generally believed to be the young man whose father worked the level crossing. How all these delicate facts were communicated from one to another of Aunt Lucy's cronies is difficult to imagine. It took me some time to understand the gist of the story, through a fog of euphemisms, when she first told me, but the legend was certainly believed and I have always thought that Roylance Cowlinshaw should have been commissioned to paint their portraits: Virgin and child and Donor. Aunt Lucy has not seen her for years but insisted on her coming up from Gloucestershire for the party. She brought her son, now 25, at whom Aunt Lucy looked with great interest whenever he was near her, as though he ought to show some signs of his peculiar origin. Poor Maud was of course there in her character of female Ancient Mariner and the chosen Wedding Guest was Murray Bassett. He, who fears boredom as others fear pain, at first looked panic-stricken but later took on the glazed and despairing look of a mouse hypnotically attached to a cat. He should have been interested in the stories, after all, they are just the sort of things people love to print in newspapers. But perhaps the dark varnish of age is visible, even to someone who has not heard them before. Mr Viot came up from downstairs with a peculiar little dog which, with his penchant for live presents, he had given to Mrs V., doped and gift-wrapped, on Christmas morning. Aunt Lucy, who considered her magnanimity in inviting him was being underrated, insisted on its being shut in the kitchen, where it ate some duck pâté and 'did its business' as Mrs Lockett put it, in a pudding basin in the bottom shelf of a cupboard. We concealed these facts from Aunt Lucy and the truce is still on, although, as usually happens in wars, the territory fought for has neither been lost nor gained. I think Aunt Lucy will let the matter of the garden rest, now that Uncle Hugo has resumed his place in the scheme of things.

Klara was in her element, handing the drinks and food and in her usual obliging way responding to each person as they required, shocked by Larry, awed by Peter Bath and Albert Minoprio, and flirting dreadfully with the Admiral. Christiane was looking very grand, in some lovely clothes that Melville had chosen for her, and *he* behaved beautifully. He was very gallant with Margot and Linda, devoted a great deal of his time to Aunt Lucy, and firmly parried the advances of Roylance Cowlinshaw, who addressed him as 'kind sir' and gave Christiane a bad moment by taking out a little notebook – but only to put down the name of the place where Melville bought his shirt. The party went on well into the small hours, presided over to the end by Aunt Lucy in the old Hartnell and her emeralds. She enjoyed herself hugely, moving about like Titania attended by her train of fairies, Spencer and three or four poets chosen specially for the occasion. Not Fishtoft, of course, who has now become merely one of Aunt Lucy's examples of villainy, the representative of Ingratitude and Double Dealing.

What an enormous letter! I am telling you all about the party, darling, because really in a way it was *your* party. Almost everybody involved in the brou-ha-ha seemed to be there, and everybody sent you their love – specially Pansy, Roylance and Albert Minoprio, who considers you as one of his successes. I thought about you a lot and talked about you as much as possible to whoever would listen.

I hope you are well and happy, darling Tigran, and having a lovely time. I am not coming to New York after all – Harvey is going to Paris as Counsellor, which is more important than it sounds. If I meet the Mouscadets in my progress through society, I will give them your kind regards. I expect we shall have a large and elegant apartment, and I hope soon to see you there. It won't be Pigpound Lane, but perhaps the next best thing. It is difficult to end; I don't want to stop talking to you. But I must, if I am to avoid having to have this letter bound and sent to you by book post. So I will just say thank you darling, and send you my love.

Your, Cornelia